CADE

A MacKenzie Novel

Liliana Hart

ISBN: **1470107163**
ISBN-13: **978-1470107161**

DEDICATION

To Dallas

Because there's no one else I'd rather go through life with. Thanks for making me a better person.

ACKNOWLEDGMENTS

To all the fans that kept asking for Cade's story. Thanks for making my job so much fun.

PROLOGUE

Miami, Two Years Ago

Cade MacKenzie knew fear.

It pressed against his chest and squeezed at his heart every time his lover screamed in pain. She stared at him out of wild eyes that had melted like dark chocolate when she'd climaxed in his arms only a few hours before. She'd been soft and pliant against him, his name a chant on her lips, as he buried himself inside her.

But now those eyes were full of terror, the bruise on the side of her face already discolored and her lips swollen and bleeding where Miguel del Fuego had taken his fist to her—a man who never showed remorse or guilt over terrorizing women or children. Carmen had been caught giving the location for del Fuego's next drug shipment to the DEA, and there were no second chances with the cartel leader. Not even for his own daughter.

Cade and Carmen had been dragged from bed in the middle of the night, both of them naked, the evidence of their passion still evident on their damp skin. They'd been blindfolded and beaten, and Cade knew without a shadow of a doubt that it was no one's fault but his own. He'd been so wrapped up in the woman, so desperate to be inside her, that he hadn't swept his room for bugs. He hadn't found one in over two years. Miguel had begun to trust him, to groom him to take over the cartel. But Cade had let his guard down and taken that trust for granted, and now they would both pay the price.

Cade knew the warehouse they'd been taken to well—the large wooden crates stacked against the walls, the oil-stained concrete, the black panel vans parked in the center of the space. He'd spent the afternoon there himself, making sure everything was in place for the shipment of Miguel's new date rape drug to come into the US from Colombia. Its street name was *Rabbit*, and it was particularly dangerous because it could be administered through the skin. One touch of the powder against a hand or the back of the neck, and the person it had been given to wouldn't care where, who or how many they were fucking. Man or woman. Even as their minds screamed no, their bodies would betray them and beg yes. If it was injected into the bloodstream, there was no chance for survival.

There had been too many deaths over the last several years because of the drug, and Cade had been selected to infiltrate del Fuego's cartel and take them down once and for all.

The warehouse was bugged and his team was aware of

the shipment coming in. It would be unloaded at the docks and brought to the warehouse for safekeeping until it could be distributed to del Fuego's suppliers. But the shipment wasn't supposed to happen for another four hours, and Cade knew there was a chance he and Carmen could be shit out of luck as far as having anyone in place for a rescue.

Cade's own wounds were severe and made it difficult to stay conscious. The gunshot wound to his shoulder bled freely—too freely—and he had at least three cracked ribs. But with every blow he received, he kept his eyes steady on Carmen's, hoping his courage would be her strength. He was proud of her. She didn't beg for mercy as she was beaten. She stared at her father with all the hatred and loathing she'd always felt for him. She'd spent twenty-two years being his prisoner, and she'd known it was only a matter of time before she became his guinea pig for the drug he was so proud of.

When Cade had gone undercover in del Fuego's cartel three years before, he'd had every intention of seducing Carmen into giving him the information the DEA needed to shut down the cartel. He'd had no problems lying to her, or spinning a future together he had no plans of delivering. But Carmen had surprised him. Her sweet, shy smiles, and her need for love had broken through every plan he'd made. The last thing he'd expected was to fall in love with her.

"I'm disappointed in you, Carmen," Miguel said, caressing the side of her swollen face with his pistol. "You've been telling my secrets to this *gringo*. To the American authorities. Your loyalty should always be to your family. *Sí?*"

Cade jerked against his captor's arms as Miguel struck Carmen again, and he fought to stay conscious as fingers dug into the wound at his shoulder.

"Stop it, *Papá*," Carmen cried, crawling toward Cade. "They're hurting him. Please don't hurt him."

"Would you have me spare this man, Carmen? A man I trusted? One I hoped would take over my business and give me strong grandchildren so I could see my legacy continue?"

"Yes. Please, Papa," she begged.

"Would you die for him, Carmen?"

"No!" Cade shouted. "This is between you and me, Miguel. Carmen's loyalties are divided. Let her go."

Cade fought again to break free of the hold they had on him, knowing what was coming, desperate to stop it. Two men weren't enough to hold him down, and two more came from somewhere, getting in punches to his cracked ribs to slow him down. He strained against their hold, sweat and blood running into his eyes, but he couldn't get to her.

"Answer me, Carmen. Is this traitor's life worth your own? Do you love him that much?"

"Yes," she whimpered, her hand reaching out to Cade as she crawled closer, her arm wrapped around her middle.

God, where was his team? They should know something was wrong. Know he needed them. Cade used the last of his strength to work his arm free and hold his hand out to Carmen, praying for a miracle. He needed to touch her, to hold her. She placed her smaller hand in his, her slim fingers bloody and broken, and Cade looked up at Miguel, ready to do whatever it took to save her. To bargain his soul if the monster in front of him would take it.

But when he met Miguel's eyes, they were mocking and full of hatred. A hatred that had no possibility of being extinguished.

"Ah, young love," Miguel said, his smile becoming crueler. "This is on your head, Cade MacKenzie."

Cade threw his body toward Carmen, but he was too late. The shot from Miguel's gun echoed in his ears along with his screams, and Carmen's hand went limp in his, her blood splattered across his face and chest. Blood he knew he'd never be clean of.

Chaos reigned around them as the warehouse went black and the shouts of soldiers and agents swarming through the building started to penetrate the haze of shock and anger. He kept waiting for Miguel to finish what he'd started and put a bullet through his brain, but it never happened. Those that held him captive ran for cover, so only he and Carmen lay in the middle of the warehouse floor, flashes of gunfire and smoke building around them.

He pulled himself closer to her body and gathered her in his arms, his mind numb with grief, and he snarled as hands tried to jerk him away from what was his.

"Dammit, Cade, look at me."

The voice in his ear was familiar, and he didn't fight as night vision goggles were placed over his eyes. His brother,

Declan, came into focus.

"I can't—," he tried to say, holding Carmen closer.

"We'll get her out, Cade. We'll do right by her," Dec said, taking her from his arms into his own. "But we need to get you out right now. The del Fuego cartel will be gunning for you."

Cade nodded and let his brother lead him out of hell, but he heard the voice that called to him over the chaos.

"You'll never be safe, Cade MacKenzie," Miguel screamed. "You'll never know peace as long as I'm still breathing. I'll take everything and more that you've taken from me."

Cade couldn't imagine what more the man could hope to take from him. His future had been the dead woman in his brother's arms.

CHAPTER ONE

Present Day

Neighbors were a pain in the ass.

Especially neighbors who made as much noise as possible at the crack of dawn. Did no one have consideration for their fellow man anymore? She wasn't asking for much, dammit. Just a little common courtesy.

Bayleigh Scott rolled toward her nightstand to look at the old fashioned alarm clock with the giant hands and noticed it was just shy of 6am. She groaned and pulled the pillow over her head, trying desperately to block out the grinding noise from what sounded like a fleet of semis outside her window. She'd closed her shop at ten the night before but hadn't gotten home until after one because she'd been doing inventory. Not even five full hours of sleep. And she had to be back to open at ten since her assistant was out sick.

When the pillow failed to have the effect she was looking for, she tossed it across the room and felt the slow flush of anger work through her body.

"Who the hell do these people think they are?" she muttered, throwing back the covers and stomping to the bay window in her bedroom.

She could only see the back deck of the house next door from her window, and she scowled as she noted the ferns already hanging from baskets on the porch, the dimmed sconces attached to the posts giving her a good view in the darkness.

"Making yourself right at home, aren't you?"

She let the curtain drop and stomped through the house, tripping over the edge of the rug and bumping her shin against the table she had at the end of the couch. The coffeepot beckoned, so she punched the button to start her morning caffeine as she made her way to the kitchen window. She had the perfect view of the neighbor's front yard.

Bayleigh winced as the screech of the truck lift going up and down assaulted her ears. It wasn't like the noise would bother anyone else. Most of her neighbors turned their hearing aids off after eight o'clock and didn't turn them back on until the sun rose. There was no way her new neighbors were another little retired couple like everyone else on the street. They were probably party animals or reprobates. Maybe both.

Powerful lights were set up so they could unload the

truck that was backed into the driveway, but all she could see was the shadows of men as they unloaded the furniture. They didn't even need that stupid lift. They were just being lazy. There was no reason for the truck to be on at all.

Muttered curses propelled her out the front door before common sense could take hold. She never did well on little sleep and no caffeine. It wasn't her fault. She liked to think of it as a medical condition. She'd just explain politely about the noise, and surely they would take care of things from there. It was the decent thing to do.

The cool October air slapped against her skin, reminding her she was only wearing the cotton boxers and tank top she'd slept in. Chills raced across her skin and she tripped over the hose that ran across her sidewalk. She'd forgotten to roll it back up after watering her flowerbeds the previous morning.

She paused for a moment, wondering if she'd made a mistake when she felt three sets of eyes look in her direction. The sudden stillness of the night was unnerving. She couldn't see the two men in the shadows clearly, but she got a heck of a glimpse of the man standing closest to her. The Devil in disguise. The sudden urge to cross herself had her squeezing her fingers into tight fists. She wasn't even Catholic for Pete's sake.

His scowl was black and menacing and he narrowed his eyes at her in warning, automatically putting her back up. She wasn't going to be intimidated by the likes of him. At least not by much.

Bayleigh straightened her shoulders and marched across

the tiny patch of grass that separated the two houses. She climbed into the cab of the big white truck, the cracked seats scratchy against the backs of her legs, and turned off the ignition before taking the key. She jumped out of the truck and watched warily as the three men gathered close, their arms crossed over their bare chests and various looks of surprise pasted on their faces. Maybe Satan was having a convention, because surely all three of these men were fallen angels of the worst kind, or hardened criminals at best.

They were muscled and bare-chested, and their jeans hung low on narrowed hips. It was obvious they were related, and her gaze passed over them all quickly. But she couldn't seem to take her eyes off the one in the center—the one who'd made her lose her common sense with just one scowl. There was something in his eyes that had her taking a step back before she remembered she was standing in the middle of a safe neighborhood. She wouldn't be intimidated on her own property. She looked down and took a quick step back so she was actually on her own property, and crossed her arms over her chest, daring him to say anything.

The Devil's dark hair was longer than she liked on a man, almost to his shoulders, and his eyes were as black as coal. Probably because he'd been hauling it in hell before he'd decided to move to Fort Worth, Texas. A short beard covered his face and a wicked looking tattoo swirled over his shoulder and part of the way down his arm. His chest was scarred, and she couldn't even begin to imagine what had happened to him to cause such marks. Her gaze lowered, following the black smattering of hair that disappeared beneath his jeans, and all rational thought left her head as she noticed the sizable bulge behind his zipper.

"You've got some mighty friendly neighbors, Cade," the man next to the Devil said, his smirk evident in the slow drawl of his voice. "She can't take her eyes off you."

Bayleigh felt heat flush her cheeks, and she brought her eyes back up to meet his. The keys bit into the palms of her hand reminding her she had them, so she tossed them to the walking hard-on a little harder than was probably necessary. He snapped them out of the air and glared in her direction, and the urge to turn tail and run was prevalent in her mind, but instead she turned around and calmly and put one foot in front of the other.

"What the hell do you think you're doing?"

She knew it was him that spoke without having to turn around. His voice slid across her skin like rough velvet, and she shivered at the demand in it. Not that she expected the Devil to be an easy man or be without a modicum of power, but she liked to think she had enough self-control to ignore the dangerous seduction of his voice and keep walking.

She eyed the distance to her front door and looked back in his direction. He'd taken a couple of steps forward, and there was no way to get away from him if he came after her. He narrowed his eyes as if he could read her mind, and shook his head slowly, warning her not to try it, so she swallowed her fear and turned around to face him.

She was an idiot. Running would have been the smart thing to do if the look on his face was anything to go by. She could have made it. Maybe.

"Most of us sleep here in the middle of the night," she

finally said with more bravado than she felt. Never let them see you're afraid. Her father had repeated the mantra constantly during her childhood. "I figured since it was your first day in the neighborhood, you might want to start out on the right foot."

"You thought wrong," he said. "And this is far from the middle of the night. The sun's already coming up. Maybe you're just lazy."

Bayleigh's eyes narrowed at the insult. She'd never been accused of being lazy a day in her life. But while her father's advice rattled around in her brain, something her mother always told her came to mind, just as it had every time she'd moved from school to school and had to deal with the inevitable "new kid" bullying.

Kill them with kindness.

So she smiled as sweetly as possible and said the only thing she could think of to strike terror into his heart.

"You know, there are a lot of elderly people that live on this street."

"So?" he growled. "And then there's you. Let me guess. You're single?"

"I've been engaged," she said, narrowing her eyes.

"I can see that worked out well for you. I take it he couldn't manage to bring himself to the altar?"

"Something like that," she said softly, the old feelings of not quite being good enough surfacing before she could tramp them back down.

"Look, I'm sorry," he said. "That was out of line. I promise I'll leave everyone on the whole damned street alone if they'll leave me alone."

Bayleigh felt the beginnings of a headache forming at the back of her skull. Between the lack of sleep and the one-two punch her new neighbor had just delivered, reminding her of her former fiancé and the myriad of inadequacies she hadn't realized she'd had until she'd met him, she decided she wasn't in the mood to be nice after all.

"Oh, no. No need to apologize. If anything it's my fault for getting in at one this morning after working a fourteen hour day," she said sarcastically. "It was inconsiderate of me to expect you to move in after the sun came up. Tell you what I'll do to make it up to you."

She smiled—a smile that her brothers would recognize as trouble. Her new neighbor must have recognized it too, because his eyes narrowed to black slits and the muscles in his arms bulged as he crossed them in silent warning.

"You don't really mean that about having everyone leave you alone," she said sweetly. "You seem like such a friendly and outgoing guy. I'll make sure to mention how great you are to everyone over the next couple of days. Before you know it, the whole street will be knocking on your door and introducing themselves. It won't be a month before you're hosting the neighborhood barbecue. You'll also be picking up prescriptions, mowing lawns, and eating macaroni salad with every meal so you won't hurt their feelings." She batted her eyelashes at him as he seemed to pale before her eyes. "Welcome to the neighborhood."

Laughter followed her into the house and she slammed and locked the door behind her. She knew it hadn't been him laughing. Dollars to donuts a smile had never cracked that face. The Devil didn't smile. It would pay to remember that. And so what if she'd been slightly attracted to him. Bad boys were supposed to be attractive to the opposite sex. It was a hormonal rule. But then he'd had to go and open his mouth.

Tears threatened to fall as she recalled his words. He'd been exactly right. She'd been engaged for over a year, and Paul hadn't been able to go through with the actual wedding. He'd liked her well enough as a friend, but she was too outspoken for a corporate attorney's wife. Her body was too curvy. Her language not lady-like enough. And how could she expect Paul to spend his life with a woman who didn't respond to him in bed?

It's not that she couldn't have orgasms. She had great orgasms with her vibrator. It was just that sometimes it took her longer to get there than her lovers had thought was reasonable. She'd just be warming up, and all of a sudden, they'd twitch and groan and it would all be over. The last date she'd been on was three years ago, and she hadn't even bothered to move it into the physical stage. The thought of disappointing anyone else had been more than enough to keep her celibate.

Paul had been a bastard. She knew that *now*. But at the time he'd chipped away at her self-esteem until she'd barely recognized the person she'd become. She barely ate, trying to slim down the curves he found so distasteful. She barely spoke, knowing if she didn't talk then nothing would come out of her mouth that would embarrass Paul. And she faked her orgasms just so he would think she was putting a little effort into their lovemaking.

She knew Paul had been a controlling prick by the time their wedding date had come around, and she thanked God every day that he hadn't shown up to the church that day. He'd saved her a hell of a lot of grief in the long run, but he'd damaged part of her, and she was still working like hell to get back to the person she really was. To not let those old doubts sneak up on her.

Bayleigh wiped away the tears that had managed to escape and padded back into the bedroom. It didn't matter what her new neighbor thought. No one had ever said the Devil was nice.

Now if she could avoid him for the rest of her life, he'd make the perfect neighbor.

***

"Oh, baby," Shane, Cade's youngest brother, said, still laughing at Cade's expense. "I think I'm in love. Are you sure you don't need a roommate?"

"Shut up and let's get the rest of this stuff inside."

Cade hefted his flat screen TV off the truck and headed inside, ignoring his brothers' laughter. He should have known they wouldn't be able to drop it. They were like pit bulls the moment they sensed weakness.

The urge to go next door and apologize for his

behavior was a heavy weight on his chest. He'd hurt her, and there'd been no need for it. When he'd mentioned being left at the altar, her face had paled and her blue eyes had lost the sparkle he'd found perversely arousing when she'd been arguing with him. It was as if the life had all but been sucked out of her. Hell, he'd actually enjoyed watching her in action. It wasn't often he ran across a man who had the courage to argue with him, much less a woman.

Cade scowled as he overheard the conversation from the other room.

"She'd never go for you, Shane," Declan said. "You're the runt of the litter." Cade thought it ironic since Shane was every bit as large as his two older brothers. "A woman with a body like that could only appreciate a real man."

And boy did she have a body, Cade thought, irritated his brothers had noticed. She was his neighbor, dammit. Didn't that mean he had some kind of claim? He shook his head in disbelief. His brothers were turning him into an idiot. He wasn't about to claim any woman.

He headed back to the truck for another load, but they followed him with their incessant chatter, as if they were women instead of warriors. It didn't matter she had the kind of body that had always been his weakness. He liked curves. No, he *loved* curves. And she had assets that would fill his hands nicely—breasts that were luscious and full and an ass that would look spectacular bent across his lap as he spanked the rounded globes until they glowed red.

Dammit. He'd be coming in his jeans if he kept up that avenue of thought. The distraction of a sexy neighbor wasn't what he needed at the moment, and she wouldn't be an easy woman to get involved with. She'd have expectations, and she wouldn't hesitate to give her opinion if he did something stupid. That is, if his first impression of her was correct—and his first impressions were always correct. The best thing he could do was stay far away, despite the erection that hadn't disappeared since she'd twitched those curves across the scrawny patch of grass between their houses.

"You know, when I was checking the security around the house last night I noticed you could see right into her bedroom from the back deck," Shane said, shaking his head in mock sympathy at Declan. "It'll be totally wasted on Iceman here. But I can certainly appreciate attributes like that on a woman. And did you see all of that hair? It's enough to make a man want to beg."

"Fifty bucks says she's not a real blonde," Declan said.

"Oh, you're on, brother. I'm sure if I stand on the deck long enough I'll be able to tell you one way or the other."

"What the hell is wrong with you two?" Cade bit out. "You're reducing yourselves to becoming peeping Toms? Just go to the nearest bar and pick up the first blonde you see. You'll be asking for a headache messing with the one next door. I can already tell she's going to be a pain in the ass."

"Not if you become a pain in hers first," Shane said, wiggling his eyebrows.

Cade's brothers were well aware of the kind of sexual appetite he had. He was the kind of man who demanded everything from his lovers. His thought had always been that there should never be anything sexual between a couple that was considered too dirty or taboo, and he stayed far away from women that didn't know the score going into an affair. There was no way in hell his neighbor wouldn't run away in horror at the things he wanted to do to her.

"And she does have a fine ass," Shane added.

"I'm going to kill you," Cade said.

Shane ignored the threat and said, "I swear there's something about her that's familiar though. I've seen her somewhere before. It's hard to forget someone that looks like she does, but don't worry, it'll come to me."

"Maybe she's on one of those *Girls Gone Wild* videos," Declan threw in.

Cade tuned his brothers out and thought about the neighbor. He'd run a background check on her, as well as everyone else on the street. Old habits were hard to break. And it wouldn't be long before Shane realized who she was.

Her name was Bayleigh Scott, and she owned a lingerie boutique in the square by the university. She was twenty-eight and came from a military family—a large family—just as he had, and one of her brothers was on the same SEAL team as Shane.

Cade knew Brady Scott in passing, and he knew her other brother, Brant almost as well as he knew his own brothers, but there was no way that either of her brothers would be happy if Cade pursued Bayleigh. Hell, he'd feel the same way if one of his buddies showed interest in his sister,

Darcy.

The agents and SEALS he called friends were too hard for women like Bayleigh and Darcy—men whose lives consisted of constant danger didn't have qualms about adventuring into the darker sides of sex, especially after coming off a mission.

The background check he'd done on Bayleigh didn't do justice to what he'd just seen with his own eyes. The file hadn't said she had a body that would make him instantly hard. His cock had almost burst from his jeans the moment she'd pranced across his driveway in those tiny shorts and thin tank top. She hadn't been wearing a bra, and even now his hands wanted to touch and his mouth wanted to taste.

She'd looked him over as thoroughly as he'd looked at her, and she'd been almost entranced by the sight of his erection. Her tongue had dashed out to lick her lower lip and he swore he almost felt the motion along his cock. There'd been interest in her eyes, no doubt about it.

It had been too damned long since he'd been laid. When the itch took over or the dreams of Carmen became too frequent, he found the nearest woman who would have him and fucked himself into oblivion, until the past was buried again and the itch was gone. It was the best he could do with the hand in life he'd been dealt. He never expected anything more, and wasn't prepared to give anything more in return. Life was sometimes a bitch that way. But the thought of going to another woman wasn't nearly as appealing as it should have been. Hell, Bayleigh Scott was already complicating his life.

***

Two hours later, the truck was unloaded and furniture was in a semblance of where it was supposed to be. Cade looked at the clock and decided there wasn't a thing wrong with having beer in the morning if you hadn't been to bed yet. He took two more into his bedroom at the back of the house and handed them to his brothers, who were putting together an enormous four-poster bed that had belonged to his great-grandmother.

"You don't have the sex life for a bed like this," Shane said, sucking on his skinned knuckles.

The bed in question was dark and ornate and had been hand-carved by his great-grandfather MacKenzie. It also had to weigh close to a thousand pounds. His Grandpop had been a hell of a carpenter. There was a large matching armoire, with a hidden panel large enough to fit a rifle and two handguns, and two nightstands that held knives sharp enough to cut a blade of grass. His Grandpop also believed that it never hurt to be prepared.

"You whine like a woman," Cade said, handing out the beers.

He went to the large window and looked out at his sloping backyard. It led to a small creek that ran behind all the houses on his side of the street, and huge trees grew from the sides of the bank. Sunlight shone through the branches and dappled across his scarred hardwood floors. There wasn't a fence between his house and his sexy neighbor's, so he was able to see all of her yard as well.

She had a hot tub under a large arbor that was shaded by thick tendrils of ivy and some kind of big bloomed flowers he'd never seen before. Candles were set out around the hot tub, and he couldn't help the slow curl of lust that wound through his body as he thought of the heated bubbles kissing her naked flesh, the candlelight glinting off her hair.

He shook his head at his undisciplined thoughts and turned his gaze to the narrow path that ran between their two houses. Finding the ability to swallow the cold beer was getting harder, and he felt his lungs close up at his discovery. If he stood at just the right angle he could see into the big bay window of her bedroom and through the ridiculous excuse for lace curtains she'd hung. She was going to kill him. He wouldn't have to wait on Miguel del Fuego to hunt him down after all. Death by lust. It was a hell of a thing to have to tell one's mother.

"I think someone's got a crush on the babe next door," Shane whispered loud enough that Cade had to roll his eyes. "Maybe we should call the police and tell them she has a peeping Tom."

Declan shook his head. "He is the police. It's a sad world we're living in when those sworn to uphold the law are the ones breaking it."

"Speaking of your new job—" Shane said.

"Were we?" Cade asked, his expression fierce.

The last thing he wanted to discuss was his new job with the Fort Worth police department. It was a ruse plain and simple, but no one was supposed to know about it but his former Director at the DEA. His experience with the agency had made the transition easy, and the police department had shuffled him straight into working Vice with little fuss, though they were suspicious of his motives for jumping ship. The only thing that had come into question was his accuracy with a weapon.

Several years before he'd been shot in the hand stopping a drug shipment from leaving his hometown of Surrender, Montana and crossing the border into Canada. His cousin, Cooper, had been working the job with him, and the bastards had gotten off a lucky shot. The bullet had passed right through the tendons in his hand, and the DEA had had no choice but to stick him with desk duty until he could prove himself useful again. He still hadn't gotten full use of his right hand back, but he'd worked his ass off with his other hand until he was almost as accurate a shot.

Then just as things had started to go his way and the DEA had handed him the assignment of a lifetime to infiltrate Miguel del Fuego's cartel, things had gone to shit and his life had fallen apart completely.

He'd spent three years undercover in the del Fuego cartel, and the DEA had given him a background sure to make him attractive to a man like Miguel. All traces of his real life and family had been completely wiped from the system, and for all intents and purposes, he was the son of Miguel's dead cartel rival, a part-time terrorist, and a full-time gunrunner. He'd been just exactly the kind of man del Fuego had wanted to breed with his only daughter. *Sick bastard.*

Cade still didn't know how his cover had been blown—how del Fuego had known to bug his room that night.

Someone had betrayed him. Once Miguel had discovered Cade's true identity and his position within the DEA, he'd had to go into deep hiding for almost two years until most of the major players in the cartel had been taken down. But del Fuego was still alive, and Cade knew they hadn't snuffed out the cartel completely.

It wasn't his problem anymore. He'd chosen a new path—a new life. The DEA hadn't wanted to let him go, but he hadn't given them a choice. This was the last job he'd ever work for the agency—though technically he wasn't working *for* them, being more of a consultant than an actual agent—and they weren't happy about it.

He fully expected for the cartel to hunt him down. Knew they'd come after him. But if Cade's plan worked out like he thought it would, then he'd be luring them right into his trap and get to take them out once and for all. Then he'd turn in his badge once and for all.

Cade helped his brothers lift the king-size feather mattress and put it on the bed frame, and he managed to ignore their silent looks to each other. He'd gotten good at ignoring the looks his family gave him every time they were together. They were worried. His time undercover in del Fuego's cartel had changed him, and there was nothing he could do to bring his old self back. He wasn't as quick to laugh or tease as he once was. There was a darkness inside of him that would never go away. Too much exposure to true evil did that to a person over time.

"This is a good move for you," Shane said, ignoring the warning look Cade gave him. "You're still doing what you love."

Not even his brothers knew that his current job was just another cover, though he had a suspicion that Declan was in on it. His brother seemed to know everything going on all the time.

"And now you have a house and a sexy neighbor," Shane said, shrugging. "It's very mature. You're thirty-six years old. It's about time you settled down."

"Enough, Shane," Cade growled, thoughts of the future and children he'd never gotten to share with Carmen clouding his vision. "I don't want to settle down in some picture perfect life of what you think would make me happy. I'll do my fucking job. I might even do my fucking neighbor. But I'll be damned if I bring some woman and a bunch of kids into the misery that is my life. You think del Fuego or his men will ever stop looking for me? My family would never be safe. I'm a wanted man."

"Bullshit, Cade," Shane said. "There have been no reports on activity again in the cartel. You're just afraid to live again. For the last couple of years you've done nothing but be miserable to yourself and everyone around you because of what happened to Carmen del Fuego. I know you loved her. But you might as well be dead the way you're living now. You're trying to get yourself killed. You think we're too stupid to know that you're setting yourself up as bait?"

Shane was always the more hotheaded of his brothers, and he never knew when to shut his mouth. Cade could see Declan shaking his head from the corner of his eye and moving into position to get between them if things got violent. And Cade knew that Dec wouldn't pull his punches if he was forced to break up a fight.

Cade had worked with his middle brother on several ops over the years, and Cade still had no idea what branch of the government Dec worked for or exactly what he did. He only knew that his brother always showed up when he needed to, and he wasn't someone to mess with.

"It's my life, Shane. They're my memories, my regrets, and it's my fucking guilt. I'll do what I need to, and I'll do the job I've been given. Even if it means I spend my last breath watching the cartel come to an end. Don't ever expect anything more from me. I don't need the hero worship you had for me as a kid. I know my duty."

"You're sure as fuck not anyone's hero anymore, Cade," Shane said. "You think it doesn't break Mom's heart every time she sees what you've become? Miguel del Fuego might be the most unimaginable bastard to ever walk the face of the planet, but even he's got life in him that you don't have. Because he has a purpose. His purpose might be to kill you, but it's a purpose all the same. What the hell do you have?"

"A brother who doesn't know when to shut up."

Shane grabbed his shirt off the floor and jerked it on, and Cade followed him into the living room, feeling the acid churn in his gut as his brother grabbed his duffle bag and slipped on his sunglasses. He wanted to stop him. To apologize. To just do—something. But he didn't say anything.

"You know what the shitty thing is, Cade?" Shane

asked as he turned back, his eyes hidden behind his glasses. "It's like your whole family died with Carmen that day. I don't know why the hell we all bother. I'm leaving on assignment tomorrow. I'll be back in country in six weeks."

Shane waved a hand negligently as he walked out the door, and Cade decided he'd be better off going to the kitchen for another beer rather than throwing something against the wall like he wanted to do.

"Are you leaving too?" Cade finally asked after Declan had been silent for what seemed like forever.

"Might as well. I've got a job coming up."

"I can't help the way I feel, Dec. And I can't change the way I am."

Cade heard Declan sigh, and his grip tightened around the bottle in his hand at the disappointment that one breath of air seemed to express.

"That's not for me to say, Cade. And I know it won't be one of us who has the power to make you feel differently. Maybe it's time to just open your mind to the possibilities of having something more. I'm not saying you have to," he said, before Cade could interrupt. "But maybe there's a chance you didn't die that day with Carmen after all, and there's a lot of life ahead of you. She wouldn't want you to do this to yourself."

Cade grunted and brought the beer up to quench his dry throat. He was just so damned tired. And empty. And lonely.

"Just be grateful Darcy and Grant aren't here to add their opinion to Shane's."

A rusty laugh rumbled from Cade's chest as he thought of his two other siblings. Grant had just gotten married and was settling in nicely with his new wife, and his sister, Darcy, was finishing up her Master's Degree and trying to figure out what she wanted to do with her life, driving everyone crazy in the meantime. One of the reasons he'd moved from Montana to Texas was because he never had any peace. Someone in the family—between his parents, siblings and cousins—was always trying to give him advice on how to get his life back together.

"Oh, believe me. I'm grateful."

Declan nodded and grabbed his own bag from the hall closet. "You've got a nice house here, Cade. It's older, and it's going to need some care and maintenance, but she's got a solid foundation. You've got a lot in common, I think."

"You know I love you guys, don't you, Dec?" Cade said, feeling the urgent need to let his brother know it. "I just need some time."

"I know. Try to stay out of trouble. We haven't heard rumbles of the cartel moving again, but my gut's been churning ever since you took this job. They'll find you, and I know you're expecting it, but shit happens. I'll be mighty pissed if you end up getting killed."

"I'll do my best."

Declan grinned, stretching the ragged scar on his right cheek into a fine white line. "And don't give the pretty lady next door too hard of a time. She's going to give you a run for your money."

"Never in a million years. Did you see the way she glared at me? No man wants that kind of grief all the time."

Declan's laughter followed him out the door. "Whatever you say. You know how to reach me if you need me."

He gave a two-fingered salute and slipped out the back door silently, through the trees in the backyard and to the car he had parked about a mile away. Declan was a paranoid bastard, and he had good reason to be. He also had uncanny instincts, and if his gut was churning then Cade could all but guarantee the cartel had found him. Perfect.

CHAPTER TWO

Guilt ate at Bayleigh as she tossed and turned in her bed the rest of the morning. There was no way she was going to get back to sleep. Not that she didn't have a good reason to be a bitch at that time of the morning. No judge in a court of law would convict her once they'd learned she hadn't had her coffee. But still, she should have shown a little more restraint, and she shouldn't have let him get under her skin. She'd paid for enough therapy to get over her self-esteem issues. And he'd apologized, though he'd looked damned angry about it.

The thought of those dark, wicked eyes had her body heating and her breasts aching. He was dangerous—the scars on his hard body the proof of the life he'd led—but despite the first impression of him that had stolen the breath from her body, she hadn't been afraid. Because as much as she hated to admit it, there was something about him that called to her baser nature. *Animal instinct.* There was no other way to explain her reaction to him.

Hell, maybe she didn't have the sense that God gave a turnip, as her brothers so often reminded her. Trouble had a tendency to follow her around, but she knew how to handle herself. Growing up as an army brat with a retired Colonel for a father, a brother who was a Navy SEAL, and another brother who worked for Homeland Security had given her the necessary tools to strike out on her own. But the man next door was trouble to the millionth degree, and she had a feeling there was nothing in her arsenal of tricks that could protect her from him if he ever got it in his mind to come after her.

God, she'd been more turned on just standing there looking at the bulge beneath his jeans that she'd ever been having actual sex with Paul or any of her previous lovers. But men who had that kind of sex appeal usually came with relationship issues, and she didn't want to deal with that. She wanted a partner. A man who could give her friendship, his devotion, his love *and* orgasms.

Maybe she was being too picky.

Bayleigh tossed the covers back and let the fan that spun overhead cool her overheated body, and the urge to skim her fingers across the sensitive tips of her breasts and down beneath the thin cotton of her boxers had her teeth gritting in frustration. Damn the man anyway for stirring up her anger and lust all in the same morning. And now she could expect to spend the rest of the day not only exhausted due to lack of sleep, but turned on as well.

Her feet hit the floor and she headed into the kitchen to make another pot of coffee. She was going to need it. The lace curtains at her kitchen window weren't there for privacy's sake. Her need to have the light come through her windows drove her brothers crazy, and they were constantly lowering the blinds they'd had installed for her every time they visited. But she felt safe in this neighborhood. Her neighbors were good people—mostly elderly—and the street itself was beautiful.

Huge oak trees lined the row of cottage style houses. The sidewalks were cracked and broken with age, and black antique lights were spaced evenly down both sides of the street. She liked that her neighbors were nosy and checked up on her, and she loved that she felt comfortable enough in this place to take soup to Mrs. Abernathy two houses down when she'd had pneumonia, or that she had a key to the house across the street so she could water the plants when Mr. and Mrs. Spillers went to visit their daughter in Alaska every summer.

This was the first place she'd been able to call home her whole life. Her parents had never settled more than a year or two in one spot when she was a kid because of her father's job in the military. But the question that was eating at her was why her neighbor had decided to move here. He didn't seem like the type for hearth and home or quiet neighborhoods.

She sipped at her coffee and stared next door. The moving truck was gone, and a Harley that looked a lot like its owner—mean and sleek and tough—sat in the driveway. His house was a 1940's bungalow and was sided with asbestos shingles. Diamond-paned windows decorated the front of the house and ivy grew riotously across every available surface. If it had been for sale when she'd been looking she would have snapped it up herself.

There were no coverings on his windows and she wondered what he was doing. If he still had his shirt off. Damn, she just wanted to look at him one more time, just to assure herself that he was completely unsuitable. She was such a liar.

"Damn," she muttered aloud as the alarm clock in her bedroom blared, letting her know she only had an hour to get to the shop.

She had a tendency to lose track of time and the alarm clocks were her way of making sure she stayed on schedule. Or at least mostly on schedule. Some days were better than others. She hurried back to the bedroom and took her coffee with her into the attached bathroom, showering quickly.

By the time she padded back into the bedroom, a towel hooked securely around her breasts, she'd resigned herself to at least giving the man next door an apology for her behavior. She'd get another look at him and appease her conscience at the same time.

Her shop, *Satin and Lace*, was an exclusive lingerie boutique in the outdoor shopping center a couple of miles from the college, and her clientele had certain expectations when they entered the glass double doors. They expected quality, sometimes exclusivity, and they always expected Bayleigh to act as if she didn't need their business to survive, which was completely ridiculous. It was a game, and she'd learned to play it well over the last four years. She also handmade some of the finer pieces the store offered, and she was damned good at it.

She dropped her towel and pulled on black lace panties and the matching bra she'd embroidered with gold thread. Sometimes the best perk of owning a shop like hers was she was able to sample the merchandise. Thigh high stockings followed and she attached them securely to the matching garter belt. She laid out a black pencil skirt—one that made her legs look a mile long—and a sexy three-quarter length azul sweater that veed enough to show a tempting amount of cleavage. It was part of her job to dress expensively, just as it was part of her job to offer her clients champagne and hors d'oeuvre's and have fresh cut flowers delivered to the shop.

Bayleigh moved to the bay window in her bedroom and peeked through the sheer lace curtains. She knew no one could see her. The trees shaded this side of her house, so her window was cast in darkness. Her window faced the new neighbor's deck and part of the master bedroom window, but he was nowhere in sight.

She was drawn to him. And damned if she could explain it.

***

Cade let out a slow breath as his neighbor moved away from the window. He almost hadn't gotten out of the way in time, but the sight of her ass in those barely there panties and garter belt had sweat trickling down his spine and his jaw clenched with desire. What the hell kind of game was she playing? No woman dressed like that unless they had seduction on the mind, and a woman wouldn't walk around in front of her windows unless she wanted someone to notice. Since he was the only one there at the moment, he had to assume he was her target.

His cock was swollen to painful proportions behind the zipper of his jeans, so he unbuttoned and unzipped them carefully, releasing his heavy erection into his hand. He hadn't been this hard in months—so hard his own touch was almost unbearable because he was too sensitive.

His balls were drawn up tight and he could see himself tearing that flimsy lingerie from her body and bending her over the little dressing table she was currently sitting at, his fist wrapped around the thick length of her hair as he pushed inside her.

He stroked himself from shaft to tip, spreading the drops of pre-cum over the swollen head of his cock. His back bowed and sweat ran freely down his neck and chest as he worked his shaft up and down, swirling his hand around the head, and then repeating the motions again slower so he didn't come too soon. The thought of how hot and tight she'd be clamped around him made his knees weak, and he braced his hand against the windowpane for balance.

"Have mercy, sweetheart," he moaned as she bent over to get the hairbrush she'd dropped on the floor.

The images in his mind shifted until he saw her on her knees before him, her mouth devouring him and her tongue driving him wild as his cock hit the back of her throat. The thought was too much and his balls tightened closer to his body and his cock seemed to swell in his hand as he pumped faster and faster. Muscles strained and his heart pounded as semen spurted in thick streams against the glass. His lungs seized and the need for oxygen didn't seem to be as important as it should have. The force of his orgasm took him by surprise. It had clearly been too long since he'd had a woman.

Shit. She was going to complicate his life, because there was no way in hell he was going to be able to stay away from her. He'd take her until they burned each other out. And he was positive whatever sparks there were between them would eventually die out. The life he led was too dangerous for a serious relationship. And he was too damaged. As long as she understood his position from the beginning they could focus on bringing each other pleasure instead of being tied down by emotions.

He also had to worry about keeping her safe. It wouldn't take long for the cartel to realize Cade was interested in Bayleigh, and starting an affair was the best way to keep her close. If he could convince her to stay at his house, it would be even better.

Cade knew Miguel's son, Carlos, would be the one heading the cartel's resurrection, and he'd be the one looking for revenge against Cade. There had been traces of *Rabbit*, the deadly drug Miguel's scientists had developed, found in different states for the past several years. The occurrences weren't frequent and so far they were contained to the southern states, but they were still there. No, it was too late to cut ties completely and leave her out of this operation. The best thing to do would be to draw her in. For her own safety. And for his satisfaction.

With that decision made, he got his breathing back under control and cleaned up the mess he'd made before hitting the shower. He didn't officially start work until the next day, but he wanted to go in and talk with his captain, get a feel for the station. Vice cops didn't work with partners, and he was grateful for it. One less person for him to drag down with him if things went to shit.

Cade dressed casually in a pair of jeans and a white t-shirt, tossing his old leather jacket over his shoulder as he grabbed the keys to his motorcycle. Boxes littered the path to the front door, but damned if he could find the motivation to start unpacking them. It could wait another day or five. It's not like he wasn't going to be here a while.

The front door locked behind him and his eyes immediately went next door. He sensed her before he saw her standing there—the light scent of vanilla clouding his brain, making him hungry for her. There was no way he could leave her alone now that she'd given him a preview of that fuck me underwear, but the wariness was there in his gut, the knowledge that he'd inadvertently drawn her into something that she hadn't had a choice about. He was a bastard for sure, bringing her closer when he should have been on the phone to her brothers, begging them to take her away and keep her safe until the cartel was brought down. But he hadn't, so it was up to him to keep her safe.

Cade's body pulsed, dark and hard with desire as his eyes raked over delicate feet in four-inch stilettos and wandered up over impossibly long legs. He almost swallowed his tongue at the way the black skirt hugged her curves and the smooth flesh of her thighs. His gaze lingered on her full breasts, remembering the delicate lace that touched her so intimately. Her nipples were hard and practically begged for his attention, and he could see the pulse beating rapidly in her throat and the slow flush of desire working its way up her chest. She wasn't unaffected by him, and he wanted nothing more than to sink to his knees in front of her and see how ready she was for him.

"Are you finished staring?" she asked, eyebrow quirked in annoyance.

"Are you?" he retorted, returning her look. "I wouldn't fight it if I were you."

"Fight what?"

"The attraction."

The laugh she snorted out had his lips quirking.

"My, don't you have a healthy ego?"

"I'm healthy all over. I've even had my shots."

Her gaze drifted to the hard-on behind his zipper, and he wanted nothing more than to touch her when he saw the need flare in her eyes. He tossed his jacket over the seat of his bike and walked across the small stretch of grass that divided their properties.

"Do you spend a lot of time spying on your neighbors through your kitchen window?" he asked, bringing the sparkle back to her eyes he'd dimmed earlier that morning. God, she was beautiful when she was mad.

Her cheeks heated and her eyes blazed like brilliant sapphires. "My kitchen window looks out on the whole neighborhood, and I don't spy on my neighbors. I was actually going to apologize for my behavior this morning, but it looks like my first impression of you was accurate. So you, whoever you are, can go back to your cave, where I'm sure you eat puppies for breakfast and toss children into deep holes. Jerk."

"Did you mean to say all of that out loud? You seem like the type of woman who was raised with better manners than that."

"Don't count on it."

Her eyes narrowed and her body practically crackled with anger. Her fists were bunched at her sides and he wondered if she was going to try and hit him. She had a hell of a temper, and damned if that didn't turn him on.

"My name is Cade. Cade MacKenzie."

"Who the hell cares? As far as I'm concerned you should be called Lucifer. You have the manners of a troll."

"And you have a hell of a temper. Maybe you should try anger management classes."

The little growl she let out made him want to push her against her Land Rover and hike that little skirt around her waist. He knew she'd be wet for him.

"I only have a temper when I'm faced with inconsiderate reprobates before dawn. Get a haircut and a job, and stop picking on innocent bystanders. This is a nice neighborhood. We won't stand for criminal activity around here."

"What does the length of my hair have to do with anything? Are you on medication?"

She took a step closer and poked him in the chest, and he felt his cock swell to impossible proportions beneath his jeans. Damn, she turned him on. If she had half this much energy in bed she would wear him out in no time.

"Stay out of my way, MacKenzie, or the next time I see you it won't be keys I'm throwing at your head."

Cade took hold of the hand that was thumping into his chest and pulled her closer, so their bodies aligned and she could feel the hardness of his cock against her belly. Her eyes widened and her pupils dilated so only a thin ring of blue could be seen. She licked her lips nervously, leaving a glossy sheen against her lipstick, tempting him like no woman had tempted him before.

"You don't want to threaten me, darlin'," he said, leaning down, giving her plenty of time to back away from his grasp.

He breathed in the scent of her arousal as his lips teased the sensitive skin along her jaw. She whimpered softly as his tongue teased her flesh. His hands rubbed in slow circles across her back.

"Why not?" she said on a sigh.

"Because I'd hate to have to arrest you." He whispered the words against her lips and drank in the shudder that wracked her body. "Mmm, you like the idea of handcuffs?"

"Pervert."

"You have no idea what I want to do to you. You'd like being tied to my bed, completely at my mercy."

He took her mouth quickly, before she had a chance to start thinking, and he realized as soon as his lips touched hers that he'd just made the biggest mistake of his life. Her mouth was every fantasy, every dream he'd ever had. Soft and silky and demanding. His tongue tangled with hers, drinking in her sighs as his fingers squeezed her ass, pulling her up and forward until he could feel the heat of her pussy through the layers of clothes they wore.

When he felt her pushing at his chest he dropped his hands and took a step back. And then one more. He was thinking of renting another truck and hauling all of his boxes to the other side of town.

Shit, he thought. When was the last time a woman had gotten under his skin so completely? Not even Carmen had made him lose control like this, and just having the thought was like being doused in cold water. Guilt ate at him, as if he were being unfaithful to her memory. Panic clawed at him as her face blurred in his mind, only to be replaced by the woman standing in front of him.

"We can't do that again," Bayleigh said, her voice shaking with desire.

He'd just been about to say the same thing, but hearing it out of her mouth left a bitter taste in his mouth. His eyes narrowed and he skimmed a finger over her swollen lips, smiling in triumph as her breath hitched and the pulse in her neck fluttered. He'd never been able to turn down a direct challenge.

"Do you want to bet money on it?"

"I don't bet." Her fists went to her hips, and he swore she was a second away from stomping her foot. "And don't ever lie to me. If you don't want to tell me what you do for a living, just say so. I can't stand liars. I dealt with enough of that from my ex-fiancé."

"He was obviously an idiot," he said, moving toward her again, unable to help himself. "If I was the kind of man who believed in settling down for the long haul and I had you in my bed, you'd better believe I'd never let you go."

His fingers skimmed along the delicate line of her collarbone, and he noticed the silvery flecks in her blue eyes as he watched them darken with arousal at his touch.

"I'm sure Paul initially thought that too," she said bitterly, pushing his hand away and taking a step back. "And then he got me into bed and found I didn't live up to his expectation. Apparently, men find it annoying when you don't put any effort into achieving your own orgasm. And if I didn't satisfy him in the bedroom, you can guarantee that I didn't satisfy him in any other aspects either."

Cade's brows rose in shock at what she was telling him. There was no way in hell this woman wouldn't be responsive to his touch in bed. She'd practically combusted in his arms five minutes ago.

"Baby, if you're not getting off it sure as hell isn't your fault. Blame it squarely on the shoulders of the asshole that didn't bother to take the time to find your hot buttons. Because believe me, when I get you into bed I'm going to explore every inch of your body until you're shooting off like a rocket."

She rolled her eyes and hit the button on her key fob to unlock the door of her Land Rover.

"I'm sure you're brilliant in bed, MacKenzie. But why don't you practice your smooth moves on someone who gives a damn? I don't have the time or the patience for you."

He laughed out loud, and the sound took him by surprise. When was the last time he'd had anything to laugh about?

"I'm looking forward to kissing you again, Bayleigh Scott," he said, heading back to his motorcycle. "Though I have a feeling we'll both be naked and heating up the sheets when the next time comes. And I'll make sure to bring the handcuffs."

He left her standing there with her mouth hanging open, her lips swollen and the slightest red flush against her neck where his beard had rubbed. Cade revved the Harley to life and sped out of the neighborhood, feeling more content than he had in a long time.

Hell, he might actually enjoy Texas after all.

CHAPTER THREE

"Stupid, insufferable—man," Bayleigh muttered as she maneuvered her Land Rover through traffic with the expertise of an Indy driver and a vocabulary that would make her Colonel father blush.

"Thinks he can just come over and kiss me like he owns me and then lie to my face. Cop, my ass."

The thought of that man upholding the law was almost laughable. None of the cops she'd ever met looked like Cade MacKenzie. No, there was something about Cade that reminded her a little of her brothers. He had layers, he was dangerous, and he had secrets. Not to mention he kissed like a god. Unfortunately, those all seemed to be traits she found attractive in a man.

No wonder she'd been a block of ice with her ex-fiancé and the two serious relationships she'd had before that. Their kisses had certainly never made every nerve ending in her body snap to attention, and they sure as hell hadn't made her almost come just by pressing against her intimately.

The fact that she wanted Cade MacKenzie to kiss her again was a moot point, and his threat of getting her naked and sweaty wasn't doing much to help her overactive imagination. Her brothers would have a fit if she brought home someone like Cade MacKenzie. They'd try to kill him, and she said try because she wasn't sure how well they'd hold up against Cade. The man's muscles had muscles.

Her cell phone chimed from her bag as she parked in the space behind her shop, and she dug around, grimacing as she saw who was calling her. Speak of the Devil. It's like her brothers had a sixth sense when she was about to get in trouble.

"I don't have time for you today, Brady. I'm about to open the shop."

"You don't have time for your favorite brother?" he asked. "I'm devastated."

"You're not my favorite. Brant is since he fixed the plumbing in my guest bathroom. Are you in country?"

"Beaten out because of a broken toilet. Story of my life. And yes, but I'm shipping out this afternoon. Just wanted to call and let you know. How are things in your neck of the woods?"

She sighed and tried not to worry about her brother. He was gone for weeks at a time, and they never heard anything from him until he was safe and sound back home. Or back home and waiting for his wounds to heal before he could go back out with his team. Having a Navy SEAL for a brother was nerve wracking.

"Things are—interesting," she said, thinking of Cade. She wasn't about to explain her new neighbor had left her in a state of arousal that was bordering on pain. "Pretty much the same as they've always been."

He was silent for a few seconds. "What's going on, Bayleigh? And don't even think about lying to me. You know I can find out if I start digging."

"Why would you think something's going on?" she asked, her irritation obvious.

"Because you can't lie worth shit, and when you're thinking of doing something you shouldn't, you change the inflection of your voice slightly."

"I do not!" No wonder she'd never gotten away with anything as far as her family was concerned.

"Bayleigh," he growled. "Are you seeing someone new? You only get secretive when you don't want us to run background checks on the men you're dating."

"I can't imagine why. You and Brant scared the hell out of Jeremy Franklin. He ended up moving to Maine."

Of course, she'd been a sophomore in college then and Jeremy had been a good eight years older, so he should have known better. Jeremy had thought she should put out after their sixth date, and he might have gotten a little rough when she'd disagreed, but she'd taken care of the problem with her knee to his groin and a solid right hook to his pearly whites. She knew how to protect herself. And there'd been no reason for her brothers to have him detained at the airport on his way back from a business trip and taken into a military interrogation room. Jeremy had barely been able to form a coherent sentence when he'd tracked her down to apologize.

"The bastard's lucky he didn't end up moving to the cemetery. And after all the losers you've managed to find, can you really blame us for having them checked out? You have lousy taste in men. Give me the guy's name."

"I'm not dating anyone right now."

"You're thinking about it then. Spill it, Bayleigh."

"You're not a damned mind reader or my conscience, Brady Scott. If I want to think about dating someone then it's none of your business."

"If you don't tell me, I'm going to call Dad. And I'll call Brant too. You know they won't leave you alone."

Bayleigh gritted her teeth and scowled into the phone, damning all the meddlesome men in her family to hell. If she didn't love them so much, she'd disown every one of them. But she knew Brady would do exactly as he'd threatened, and then she'd really be in trouble.

"You're a pain in the ass," she said, sighing.

"But you love me anyway. What's his name?"

"He's my new neighbor, and I haven't decided if I like him or not so there's no need to worry. He's kind of a pain in the ass, too. Maybe I should introduce you."

"His name, Bayleigh," he said with infinite patience. "I'll have time to run the background check before I ship out."

"Fine. Do your stupid background check. His name is Cade MacKenzie."

The silence on the other end of the line was so complete she thought they'd lost their connection. "Brady? Are you there?"

"Son of a bitch," Brady growled. "Tall guy, long black hair, a couple of tattoos?"

"Yeah, you can't possible know him. The world isn't that small."

"Oh, I know him. His brother is one of my best friends. But Jesus, Bayleigh, you sure know how to stick your neck into the middle of things. Cade MacKenzie is no one to mess with. My advice is to stay as far from him as possible. You don't want to get dragged into agency business. Not to mention the rumors I've heard about that man's sex life. You've got no experience with men like MacKenzie. And no, I won't tell you the details," he said before she could open her mouth to ask.

"He's already got one dead lover on his conscience. I'd hate for him to add you to it."

"What? What agency business? What dead lover?" Bayleigh laid her head against the steering wheel as her imagination ran wild. Who the hell had moved in next door to her? Rambo?

"He's former DEA," Brady said. "But whatever he's doing now, don't doubt for a second that he's not still involved in the agency somehow. The word on the street is that he officially resigned, but I don't think that's true. He's working a job. Make sure he doesn't drag you in the middle of it."

"What about the dead lover? Did he kill her?" she said, wondering if she really did have the worst judgment ever when it came to men.

"No, of course not," Brady said with enough shock in his voice for her to know he was telling the truth. "He'd never hurt a woman. But the situations he puts himself in make life dangerous for anyone connected to him. I actually like the guy, but damned if I want him sniffing after my baby sister. The man is hell on women."

"I'll remind you once again that this is my life. Maybe I'm the one doing the sniffing. I'm a big girl, Brady. And if you tattle to Dad and Brant, I'm going to let it slip what you were doing with Mrs. Haverston your senior year of high school."

"Brat," he said affectionately. "I'll keep Cade MacKenzie to myself. For now. But if you get into trouble I want to know. One of us will be there to help you."

"I'll be fine," she promised.

"Listen, I've got to go. My ride's here. Watch your six, little sister."

"Only if you promise to watch yours."

"I always do."

She didn't know how long she sat in the car after Brady hung up, her hands limp in her lap. So her first impression of her neighbor was accurate. Cade MacKenzie was a dangerous man who'd bring her nothing but trouble. Unfortunately, despite her brother's warnings, she wanted nothing more than to kiss him again. It was like telling her chocolate would make her fat. That didn't make it any less tempting.

Bayleigh grabbed her bag and unlocked the back door to her shop, flipping on the lights and putting on a pot of coffee. A knock sounded at the door, and she unlocked it long enough to receive the delivery of fresh Danishes and fruit for her morning clients. She kept an account with the bakery just a few stores down, just like she kept an account with the florist on the other side of the square. Women who spent as much money as they did in her store expected every creature comfort, and she was more than happy to give it to them.

Between her new neighbor and her brother's call, she was running more than a little behind schedule, and she quickly set out her sketch books and the fabric samples she thought her first client might like in the conference room. Becca Whitson knew exactly what she was looking for and had very traditional tastes.

The bell over the door chimed precisely at 10:30.

"Becca," Bayleigh called out in greeting, taking the young bride's hands in her own warmly. "It's so great to see you again. Come on back to the conference room. I have everything set up for you there."

Becca's smile was bright enough to light up the room, and Bayleigh remembered why she'd liked the girl so much when she'd first come in the shop. Becca was only twenty-one and had just graduated from college at the end of the summer. She came from a wealthy family and she was classically beautiful—long golden hair, bright green eyes and an innate sense of style that those of her class seemed to be born with—and she was determined to get married to her fiancé before the end of the year was out. That meant Bayleigh would have a lot of work to do if Becca chose exclusive, hand-made pieces.

"I'm so excited to see what you have for me," Becca practically gushed. "I want to knock Chris's socks off on our honeymoon."

"You'll definitely do that with what I have in mind."

For the first time since Cade MacKenzie had disturbed her sleep, Bayleigh was able to keep herself distracted through work. But when she slid the expensive lace, satins and silks through her fingers, she couldn't help but wonder if he was a man who'd enjoy his woman wearing something so blatantly carnal.

CHAPTER FOUR

"Captain Kelly," Cade said, shaking the hand his superior held out to him. "I thought I'd come in a day early, just to check things out."

Mick Kelly was a twenty-five year veteran of the force and didn't put up with anyone's shit. He barely came up to Cade's shoulders, his khaki pants bagged on him, he had a coffee stain down the front of his shirt, and his red hair was streaked through with wiry gray, but Cade had done his research, and Mick Kelly had been a damned good detective in his day. Now he was damned good at being the boss, and this job wouldn't be easy to pull over on him.

"I was just about to call you in, MacKenzie. Come into my office for a few minutes."

Cade arched a brow at the order, considering he wasn't even official for another twenty-four hours, but he followed behind him. Captain Kelly's office was a big glass cube in the middle of the precinct, and they wove their way through haphazard metal desks filled with paperwork and empty Styrofoam coffee cups before Kelly ushered him inside the cramped space.

The floor was industrial grade carpet and a dead plant sat in the corner, but Cade felt at home. Cops and agents of all kinds were inherently the same—the job always came above comfort—and he realized he'd missed the badge more than he thought he would. The last few weeks off had left him restless. He took the seat across from Kelly's desk as his captain sat in the scarred leather chair behind it.

"I want you to take a look at these. Homicide sent me the photos this morning, though the murder happened three nights past. After the investigation stalled, they decided it might be more up our alley. And after reading the reports, I tend to agree."

Kelly pushed the file across from him but kept his fingers on it until Cade looked up at him in question.

"I want you to know the DEA sent me your file," he said, doing such a complete 180 in the conversation that Cade wondered what the hell was really going on.

"The DEA seems to think you're only on loan to me for a little while. They're expecting you to come crawling back when you get tired of being confined to one space for too long."

Kelly arched a wiry brow in expectation, and Cade had to fight back the grin. The only way he'd convinced the DEA to release him was to promise them he'd be available for occasional consulting work if they needed him. He had no plans to belong to anyone after this mission was over, but Captain Kelly was liable to get more than he bargained for in hiring Cade, because he had a feeling the DEA wasn't going to let him go easily.

"Yeah, son, that file was damned interesting," his captain continued. "Though there was a lot of missing information. Anything you need to tell me? Like why the DEA is suddenly my new best friend?"

Cade met his gaze evenly, giving none of his thoughts away. The DEA could play games if they wanted to. He was retired from the agency, and all he cared about was the job he was supposed to do here. His neck had been itching and his gut churning ever since he'd crossed into Texas. And Captain Kelly was nobody's fool, though Cade knew he'd lie to the man if he had to.

"You're a tough son of a bitch, MacKenzie. Your superiors say you were an agent that always got the job done, no matter what it took. I'm giving you a hell of a lot more leeway than the other cops under my watch, but I'm going to be mighty pissed if you go back to the DEA after this is over. I'd like to have a man with your experience on the force permanently. Do we understand each other?"

Cade nodded sharply, and Kelly relaxed in his seat.

"Tell me what you see in the homicide report."

Cade pulled the file onto his lap and flipped it open, his expression never changing at the gruesome photos that lay on top. The girl was young, no more than eighteen or twenty, and her eyes stared open and blank—death a surprise on her fragile features. Makeup was smeared under her eyes and across her lips, and Cade took in the bites and abrasions on her nude body.

The syringe that stuck out of the vein in her arm might as well have been saying "fuck you" to whatever officer first arrived on scene. It couldn't have been more obvious that the girl was murdered. He read the homicide detective and medical examiner's reports, but he already knew what he'd find. He'd seen it before. This was a cartel killing, and the small cut on the inside of her thigh meant that she was the first victim they'd claimed.

The victim, her name was Katie Ross, had left one of the nicer college bars with a group of men under her own free will. The camera feed from the bar had shown that damning evidence, but not ten minutes before she'd left, she was sitting quietly at a corner table with some friends. She hadn't danced with anyone, and she'd only had one beer. But her entire personality changed after she came back from a trip to the ladies room. And video showed any number of men passing by her that could have wiped the drug across her skin.

"We need to look back at the surveillance tapes and see if there was anyone wearing gloves inside the bar," Cade said absently. "Even a tiny amount on the skin can affect whoever is administering it. Though if they wore surgical gloves it could be difficult to see in the low lighting."

After her trip to the bathroom, the girl hit the dance floor and didn't slow down. She'd gotten a lot of attention from the men—a pretty girl tempting every man in the room, obviously on the prowl. Even the bouncers had noticed her. She'd left with six guys, to the complete confusion of her friends, even though they'd tried to stop her. One of Katie's girlfriends had tried to pull her into her car to get her away from the men, but Katie had pushed her friend to the ground and gone on with the men who'd drugged her. It had been too late for her at that point. With the drug in the system, all logical thought ceased to exist. The only thing that mattered was sexual release.

One of the guys she'd left with had to be the one who'd given her the drug, but all of their faces had been averted from the cameras and they'd been unrecognizable, which meant they'd known the location of the cameras before they'd ever stepped foot inside the bar. The parking lot cameras didn't help, as the van the men and girl had piled into had bogus plates and it was as nondescript as you could get. They'd planned the whole operation very well. It was slick from beginning to end.

The girl had been taken to a pay by the hour motel less than a mile from the bar, and the medical examiner had found ejaculate from more than a dozen men. The others had probably already been waiting in the room. She'd been raped and sodomized repeatedly, and the girl hadn't been used lightly. But there were no signs of a struggle. That was the terrible thing about *Rabbit.* They'd never find signs of a struggle, even though the victim knew what was happening to her wasn't her choice.

The drug had been described by one of the victims they'd rescued in Miami as floating outside your body, watching yourself do things you knew you'd never do, and screaming silently until you thought your head would burst from the pressure. It was like being trapped in a mental straitjacket while your body went on a free-for-all without you. It was the missing signs of struggle that made it most difficult for those investigating the case, because it was made to look as if it were consensual. Unless you were familiar with the drug and what it did, and most local cops weren't even aware it existed.

"Jesus," Cade said, sickened just as much as he had been the first time he'd seen what the drug could do.

"This is some terrible shit, MacKenzie. I had no idea what it was until your former employer informed me."

Cade just grunted and kept reading. When the men had finished with the girl they'd given her an injection of the drug, ensuring her death. Miguel del Fuego's scientists still hadn't been able to stabilize the drug so it didn't have such a high fatality rate when taken internally. It was something he knew they were still working on in Colombia. Unfortunately, after Cade's true identity had been discovered, Carlos del Fuego had the compound bombed and they'd moved their headquarters. The DEA still didn't know the location of del Fuego's scientists.

"The ME says he found traces of an unidentified stimulant in her bloodstream," Kelly said once Cade closed the file. "Also high traces of progesterone and testosterone, and something the ME couldn't identify. A plant of some kind."

"It's the Yatamala root," Cade said. "It's indigenous to Central America, specifically Colombia."

Cade tossed the file back on the desk in disgust. Anger, hot and vicious, swept through his body. He wanted nothing more than to find those scientists and destroy every one of them—a bullet through the brain was too easy a death. But he wasn't with the DEA anymore, so someone else would have to kill the scientists. His job was here and the cartel had followed him. He made himself sit back in the chair and meet Kelly's eyes. He'd always had an inordinate amount of self-control.

"They call it *Rabbit* on the street," Cade explained. "The last I heard, there's only been one other documented case of the drug being used in the state of Texas. Most of it's concentrated in the Miami area, as well as along the Gulf Coast because of the location of the cartels. But a drug like this is highly desirable on the black market, and if money isn't an option then it's easily attainable if you know who to contact. It sells for a quarter million an ounce."

Kelly let out a low whistle and drummed his fingers on his desktop. "We need to find out who's supplying that drug in our state, and where it's coming from."

"I have my suspicions, sir," Cade said. "The del Fuego cartel has been waiting for me to become visible again. I'm afraid I'm the reason they're here killing innocent girls."

"They're here because they're crazy sons of bitches. And you're the one who's going to stop them. You'll stay in contact with the investigating agents in the DEA since you're known to them. They made sure to let me know that they wanted you working on this. But they said they won't interfere unless you need them. Keep me in the loop, MacKenzie. I don't want any federal surprises, but I'm giving you free reign."

"Are you sure you want to do this, Captain Kelly? Innocent men could die. This could get a hell of a lot more dangerous than you thought when you agreed to bring me on."

"I know that, son. I didn't fall off the turnip truck yesterday. But this is my city, and that drug is out there whether you think you're the reason or not. A drug like that would get here eventually, and you know it. We're just nipping it in the bud before it can spread anywhere else."

"Yes, sir," Cade said with a sigh.

Maybe when the cartel was taken down once and for all he'd go back to the stretch of land he had in Montana and retire for good. He was damned tired of trying to save the world.

Captain Kelly took out a gun and badge from his desk drawer and slid them to Cade. "Looks like you get to start a day early. Welcome aboard, son. And when this is over and the cartel is taken down, I want you to remember what a nice guy I am and come and work for me for real."

The look Kelly sent him made Cade realize he and the DEA hadn't fooled the man for a minute, and Cade nodded in respect. He took his weapon and badge and grabbed the file on the desk before heading back into the chaos of the precinct.

"Oh, and MacKenzie," Kelly called out before he could escape. "Remember I've read your file. You're a bit unorthodox to say the least. Try not to piss anyone off for at least a day or two. I really hate having to talk to the Chief."

Cade smiled, his grin a bit piratical. "Too late. You should have seen the reaction my new neighbor had when she met me."

CHAPTER FIVE

The man was making her crazy.

He'd lived next door to her for four days, and her nerves were strung so tight she was surprised her brain didn't leak right out of her ears. He had a habit of showing up out of nowhere, and she'd gotten to the point where she was sneaking in and out of her house like a thief just to avoid him. Because damn, that kiss could *not* happen again. He'd have her naked and on her back in no time if his lips ever touched hers again. And she wasn't about to let that happen.

Common sense had kicked in once her brain had started functioning again. Cade had actually said, "If I was the kind of man who believed in settling down for the long haul," which meant he wasn't the type at all. She wasn't built for one night stands or casual affairs. It wasn't his fault, it's just the way she was. But she also knew the power of attraction. She was only human, but as long as she stayed away she'd be fine.

"You okay, Bayleigh?" her assistant, Tara LeCourt asked. "You've been acting strange all day. Maybe you're coming down with that same bug I had."

Tara's smooth mocha skin was creased with concern, her dark eyes filled with worry, and Bayleigh turned back to the mannequin she was working on in the window so Tara wouldn't see the lie on her face.

"I'm fine, Tara," she said, adjusting the black lace negligee so it hung perfectly. "Just a little tired. I haven't been sleeping well the last couple of nights."

The long swath of fabric was completely sheer, shot through with threads of silver. The neckline and back plunged dramatically, and it was meant to catch the eyes of those walking past her shop. All she could think about was wearing it for Cade and watching him lose his mind. Of course, she'd have to alter the bust if she were to wear the gown, but it would be worth the extra work.

"Well, it's no wonder. You've worked non-stop since I was out sick. I still think you need to hire a part-time person or two. We're getting enough business that you and I are spread pretty thin. And it would be nice to have extra time off every once in a while."

"I know. I just want it to be the two of us for as long as possible. I'm not ready to let go just yet."

She and Tara had met in college and had been inseparable ever since, and the thought of someone else coming in made her heart hurt just a little. She'd built her business from the ground up, and it was making her a hell of a profit. To the point that she'd started to think about opening another shop in Dallas.

"Why don't you go home for the rest of the day?" Tara said. "And take tomorrow too. I'm feeling much better, and you look like you need the—"

Tara's words trailed off as the bell chimed over the front door, and she could have sworn she heard her friend mutter, *Holy Mother of God* under her breath. Bayleigh knew it was him before she turned around. The atmosphere was immediately charged with tension, and she swore her nipples hardened like homing beacons whenever he was near.

Bayleigh gave the front window display a final look before turning to Cade. She made sure her expression was composed and her breathing was mostly normal before she met his eyes.

"I don't think we have anything in your size here, MacKenzie."

Tara choked and Cade smiled wickedly, making Bayleigh's heart pound harder in her chest.

"What do you have in your size?" he asked "This?"

His fingers skimmed the bodice of a silvery blue gown she'd been eyeing for herself. It was more modest than most of the pieces in the shop, but it was breathtaking, reminding her of something that would have been worn in the forties.

"I think I'm going to take my lunch break," Tara said wide-eyed. "Three is obviously a crowd here." She grabbed her purse from under the counter and headed out the door before Bayleigh could stop her.

"You've been avoiding me, Bayleigh."

"I know, Cade," she answered sardonically, causing his lips to twitch.

"I didn't take you for a coward."

Her eyes narrowed and she took two steps forward before she realized that's exactly the reaction he'd wanted her to have. She was too close to him now—so close all he had to do was reach out and pull her into his arms.

"I'm not a coward. But I'm also not stupid. You think I didn't see the light that went off in your eyes when I told you I couldn't have an orgasm. All you want is the challenge of trying to prove me wrong."

"That's not all I want from you, baby."

"Really? So you're interested in taking me out to dinner? Maybe to a movie? Getting to know each other over bad Chinese food and neighborhood barbecues?"

Cade's eyes narrowed and she knew she'd struck home with her point. He wanted her in bed and nowhere else. He didn't want the connection of anything past the physical.

"We've known each other four days," he said. "Don't you think you might be overreacting a little?"

"No, I don't."

He took a step toward her, and it was everything she could do to hold her ground. His fingers touched her hair lightly before moving to the sensitive skin at the side of her neck. She gasped at the contact and she felt the dampness gather between her thighs. Chills snaked up her spine and zinged across every erogenous zone in her body.

"What's wrong with satisfying the physical aspect? Those needs and feelings will always be there. We can be friends later. Once the edge is off and our bodies are sated. What's wrong with giving in to that need? Sex is just another part of life. Why would you deny yourself one of its greatest pleasures?"

Confusion began to cloud the lust rioting through her body. He made a persuasive argument, one she was tempted to give in to. But it wasn't just her need for something more that was holding her back. It was shame. And fear. What would happen when he finally got what he wanted? Would he be disappointed when she didn't respond the way he imagined? Would he look at her with disdain and tell her all the things she was doing wrong? It wasn't a chance she was sure she could take. Paul had damaged her pride, but she had a feeling Cade could destroy it completely.

"In my opinion, I'm not denying myself anything," she said, shakily.

"Only because you haven't had me inside you yet."

He leaned down and took her mouth fast and hard, his tongue sliding along hers sinuously, and she realized too late that the moan she'd heard had come from her.

He pulled back, but he kept her wrapped loosely in his arms. "What's going on between us is rare, Bayleigh. I don't think you're experienced enough to realize how rare. It's fine that you want something more, and I won't stand in your way when you're ready to find it, but there's no reason we can't enjoy this and take advantage of it while it lasts."

"You're asking a lot of me, Cade. I just don't know if I can do it."

"We'll see, sugar."

He kissed her again, and she melted into his arms, knowing her resistance was wearing thin. If he kept up this assault she'd never be able to hold out against him.

"Oh, sorry," Tara said as she came back in the shop.

Bayleigh hadn't even heard the chime ring, but she could tell by the smug look in Cade's eyes that he'd been perfectly aware of what was going on.

"I thought you'd be done by now." Tara's eyes danced with humor as she moved back behind the counter to store her purse. "Who's your friend, Bayleigh? And why am I just now finding out about this? You've got a lot of explaining to do, girl."

Bayleigh stepped out of Cade's embrace and narrowed her eyes at him. "There's nothing to explain. He's a nuisance. And my new neighbor," she added as an afterthought, waving her hand agitatedly.

"Cade MacKenzie," he said to Tara, his mouth quirking as if he wanted to laugh.

Bayleigh was glad they were both having such a good time at her expense.

"New neighbor, huh?" Tara asked. "So you bought the house Bayleigh wanted."

"Really?" Cade asked, his curiosity evident in his expression. "Why didn't you buy it?"

"Because it wasn't for sale then. And I love my house. Will you please go away now and stop bothering me?"

"Sure," Cade said. "I can always bother you at home later. I've got to get back to work anyway."

It wasn't until he'd mentioned it that Bayleigh noticed the silver badge hooked to his belt and the sidearm he had strapped at his waist. He had the ability to cloud her judgment and her senses just by being in the same room. He hadn't been lying. He really was a cop.

She swallowed painfully, looking at the evidence in front of her face before meeting his laughing eyes. "So I guess you really are a cop?"

Tara burst out into laughter, and Bayleigh scowled at her friend.

"Want to see my handcuffs?" Bayleigh felt the heat rush to her cheeks at the memory of what he'd promised to do with those cuffs and she straightened her shoulders, more determined than ever to keep pushing him away.

"Goodbye, Cade."

"Goodbye, Bayleigh," he mimicked in the same tone of voice and winked as he left her shop.

"Helloooo? Bayleigh?" Tara said, waving her hand in front of her face to get her attention. "You want to tell me what's going on?"

"Nothing is going on. That man is driving me crazy."

"He's obviously doing a good job of it. I've been trying to get your attention for a good five minutes."

"I think I'm going to go home," Bayleigh said.

The sensations pulsing through her body made it difficult to function, much less think. There was no way she'd be any help in the shop for the rest of the day, and she didn't have any appointments scheduled that needed her personal attention.

"Good, why don't you take that blue silk gown with you? Your new neighbor seemed partial to it."

"You're not helping, Tara." Bayleigh grabbed her purse and the light sweater she'd worn that morning, trying to remember where she'd put her car keys. Tara reached into the drawer under the counter and handed them to her.

"What were they doing in there?" Bayleigh asked.

"You tossed them in there when you were looking for an envelope," she answered. "You know he's not going to leave you alone until he has what he wants. That man has Alpha written all over him. I don't suppose he has a brother, does he?"

"Three, I think. I'm sure the Neanderthal runs in the family."

"As long as he's good in bed, then I can do without the stimulating conversation for a while."

Bayleigh hmmmed noncommittally, wondering if her need for stimulating conversation and friendship was because she'd never had the satisfaction in the bedroom. Maybe she was looking at this all wrong. Or maybe she was looking for any excuse at all to give herself permission to give into Cade's demands.

***

She spent her afternoon off watching old movies and working on some of the exclusive pieces Becca Whitson had ordered, thinking of the day she'd be able to design her own pieces. She decided being alone with her thoughts for the afternoon had left her nothing but confused and wanting. Her body was primed and damned if her vibrator was taking the edge off like she needed it to.

She'd finally thrown on a pair of old pajama pants and an old Texas Rangers jersey and decided to call it a night when the doorbell rang. It was well after nine o'clock at night, and she rarely got visitors this late unless one of her neighbors had an emergency and needed help. She grabbed her robe and was just tying it when she answered the door.

"Nice robe," Cade said, eyeing her from head to toe before stepping inside as if he owned the place. "I've never seen flannel in a patter quite like that before."

"Umm, you can't just come in without an invitation."

"You invited me earlier today," he said, tossing a DVD in her direction as he roamed around the house, looking things over, and mentally dissecting her decorating choices. "You asked if I wanted to watch a movie. Here I am."

"Porn doesn't count," Bayleigh said, rolling her eyes as he went to all of her windows and began lowering the blinds.

"I wouldn't bring porn. At least not on the first date."

"So this is your idea of a date?"

She followed him into the living room and watched as he dropped down on the couch and picked up the remote. He should have looked ridiculous against the delicate floral pattern of her too small couch, but instead it just showcased his maleness—the power and energy that seemed to come off of him in waves.

"Nah, this is just two neighbors getting to know each other. Do you have popcorn? Also, haven't your brothers told you that it's not safe to let people see in your windows? You have blinds, woman, use them."

"How do you know I have brothers?"

"It's a trade secret, sweetheart. If I told you, I'd have to kill you."

"Oh, please," she said, wondering how she'd lost the upper hand.

And where the hell was she supposed to sit? He practically took up all the space on the couch.

"And yes, my brothers tell me to use my blinds every time they come to visit, but I ignore them just like I'm going to ignore you. I moved here because of how beautiful the street is, not to hole up in my house like a paranoid ex-DEA agent who expects the whole world to be out for him."

"How do you know I'm an ex-agent?" he asked, eyes narrowed.

"Trade secret, sweetheart," she said, smiling serenely. "If I told you, I'd have to kill you."

He threw his head back and laughed and the sound caressed her already sensitive nerve endings. She should throw him out and bolt the door behind him. She'd never be able to resist him if he created something more than just physical between them.

"So are you going to join me over here or stand there all night with your mouth hanging open? Though I have to say, the bathrobe is a pretty great deterrent for what I originally had in mind. I thought you'd be more inclined to wear the things I saw in your shop."

"Only in your dreams, MacKenzie."

Bayleigh put in the DVD and went to join him on the couch, trying not to dwell on the fact that she fit perfectly in his arms.

"Don't think you're going to break me down by being nice all of a sudden," she said. "I'm on to you, mister." She propped her bare feet on the coffee table and ignored the heat that seemed to leap between them every time they touched. "And next time I get to pick the movie."

CHAPTER SIX

"I'm going to kill him," Bayleigh said as she rolled out of bed a week later, the morning light of dawn barely peeking through her windows.

Cade had generally made himself a pest for the past week. He'd shown up at her house late every night, looking ragged and tired, and she could see a glimpse of something dark and sad in his eyes—something that seemed to be growing in intensity—but he never brought it up, and she wasn't going to ask. He worked erratic hours and something was eating at him.

Their "friendship" was tenuous at best. They'd watched a couple of movies, but they'd spent most of the time debating and arguing anything and everything they could think of. And boy did they argue. It was the best damned foreplay she'd ever had, and she'd shoved him out the door angry more nights than she'd let him stay just to preserve her sanity.

As much as she hated to admit it, she was surprised to find he stimulated her mind almost as much as he stimulated her body. And he'd taken plenty of opportunities to remind her that the chemistry between them was still there and going strong.

Her brother's words had haunted her for the past two weeks. She wanted to know about the lover Cade had lost. What he was really doing in Texas. And she wanted to know why he wasn't pushing the physical aspect of their relationship anymore. He still kissed her every chance he got, but he'd stopped filling her head with the descriptions of what he wanted to do to her. Of how it would be between them.

Doubts that she'd done something wrong had begun to creep in on her the last couple of days, and as much as she tried to tell herself that it didn't matter, she found that it did matter. She wanted that connection between them. To know that she was special and could incite that kind of reaction in a man. And she wanted a non-self-induced orgasm, dammit. She had a feeling that if any man could give her one, it would be Cade MacKenzie.

She'd found out over the last several days that all the neighbors had begun to pay visits to Cade. Mrs. Spillers from across the street had taken him a casserole, and Bayleigh had been fascinated to know that he'd invited her in and they'd talked over coffee for a few minutes.

She'd gone across the street the next evening while Cade was out on a call to fish for the details, since she couldn't imagine Cade having the manners to entertain an eighty-two year old woman for more than five minutes. But

Mrs. Spillers had been sighing like a teenager the whole time she talked about him.

"Have you ever seen a man with eyes that dark?" she said, cutting a slice of the coffee cake Bayleigh had brought over and setting it on the kitchen table where she was sitting. "It was like he could see right into my soul. If I was fifty years younger, I'd take him for a wild ride."

Bayleigh choked on her coffee cake and took a long drink of tea to clear her throat. The thought of Mrs. Spillers—her hair curled in steel grey sausage rolls and her skin slack over her bones—taking anyone for a wild ride was just a little disturbing.

"He can probably see to your soul because he doesn't have one himself. He's probably looking for a good one to steal."

"Bayleigh Scott, that's a terrible thing to say about such a nice young man. You could do a lot worse than someone like Cade MacKenzie. He even offered to patch the spot on the roof by the chimney so the rain doesn't keep leaking in. I hope he takes his shirt off when he fixes it," she said, fanning her face with her hand. "It's been a long time since Mr. Spillers looked like that."

Bayleigh was willing to bet Mr. Spillers had never looked like that. Mr. Spillers was barely five foot eight in his dress shoes and he couldn't weigh more than a hundred pounds soaking wet. Though she couldn't blame Mrs. Spillers for wanting to see Cade's muscles. Bayleigh wouldn't mind seeing them again either.

She listened to Mrs. Spillers wax poetic about Cade's good manners and the muscles in his arms for another forty minutes before she excused herself and went back home, hornier than hell and jealous that Cade had managed to have a long conversation with another woman without insulting her. Apparently, it was only Bayleigh that brought out the worst in him.

There had been plenty of opportunities to admire his physique over the two weeks since he'd moved in. Sometimes at night, after he'd left her house, he stood out on his back deck, a beer in hand and his gaze lost in the trees behind their houses, his shirt off and his jeans unbuttoned just enough to drive her crazy. She always made sure her light was out, and she knew he couldn't see her watching him, but she couldn't help but skim her fingers across her nipples, tweaking them to hard points and wishing it was his hand, his mouth. He was a fever that wasn't going away, and his nightly visits were just making it worse.

Shame washed over her as he became the object of her fantasies. While he was lost in thought next door, minding his own business, her body was heating and her pussy flooding with a need she'd never experienced before. Her vibrator had gotten more use in the past two weeks than it had in the last six months.

She tried to resist the temptation, but she'd ultimately end up spreading her thighs, moaning as the thick vibrator filled her—wishing for Cade. But even after orgasms strong enough to make her scream, satisfaction still didn't find her. Not completely. She'd never been able to come with a man inside her, and she longed for Cade to be the one who finally proved to her that she wasn't frigid after all. She needed him to show her that it wasn't she who was deficient. That it wasn't she who was lacking.

Bayleigh shook off the memories as an unholy sound assaulted her ears.

"Damn," she swore as the cold wood floors bit into her feet.

No matter how attracted she was to the man, there was no way she was going to let him interrupt the one day she had off. Waking up at dawn hadn't been on the agenda for her Sunday. A late breakfast, a little shopping, a chat with her parents on the phone. Those had been her plans for the day. Not being shaken out of bed by Led Zeppelin blaring into her room and rattling her windows.

She didn't bother to put on a robe or comb her hair as she marched across her front yard to the house next door. Her pajama pants were wrinkled and her t-shirt was threadbare. Her mother would be mortified if she could see her daughter now. A southern woman didn't leave her house without the proper clothes and her face made up. It was one of those rules that ranked right up with never leave the house without clean underwear on just in case you're in a wreck.

Cade's Harley was parked in the driveway and his garage door was open. He stood with his back to her—*God, why couldn't the man ever wear a shirt?* And he was bent over the hood of his truck, using some kind of tool as if he actually knew what he was doing. She had a grade-A view of his terrific ass, and the sight threw her off her stride for just a minute. But a guitar riff that caused the hairs on the back of her neck to stand up let loose and she remembered her purpose.

He didn't notice her standing behind him with her hands over her ears, so she went to the stereo in the corner and turned the volume all the way down. Her ears rang in the immediate silence and she found satisfaction as his head came up and bumped the open hood of the truck. Served him right.

By the narrowing of his eyes, he must have read her mind. Or maybe she'd actually said that out loud.

"You know, I'm getting damned tired of you turning my shit off. You're the nosiest neighbor I've ever had."

"I'm sorry, I can't hear you. I'm as deaf as Mr. Lowenstein on the other side of you."

He straightened and wiped his hands on the rag he had tucked in his back pocket, shooting her a black look she would have paid more attention to if she hadn't been so angry.

"And do you know what I'm getting damned tired of?" she asked, her heart thumping wildly in her chest as he tossed the rag to the ground and came toward her. She couldn't decide if the look in his eyes meant he wanted to kiss her or strangle her. "I'm getting tired of being woken up at the crack of dawn just because you have a wild hair up your ass to do whatever the hell it is you do at that ungodly hour. I've put up with you mowing your lawn, using a nail gun, and revving your motorcycle all before the sun is barely in the sky. Some of us work for a living, buddy."

"Would it kill you to use my name once in a while? I thought we were past this. I bet I know how you could get rid of some of that tension you're carrying around," he said with a smirk.

"Are you planning on moving?"

He shook his head in pity. "You'd miss me if I left. Admit it. You've gotten used to having me around. Who else would you get to watch all those terrible girly movies with you?"

"Can we get back to the subject please? I'm trying to sleep. Not all of us work the insane hours you do. I like routine."

"Bullshit. You like to think you like routine, but you thrive in chaos, sweetheart. Besides, Tara works for you on Sundays, though she didn't last week because she was sick."

"How do you know that?"

"I've heard it from every damned person on the block whenever they've dropped off brownies, sponge cake and casseroles. The consensus is that you work too much and don't have near enough fun. Your sex life is non-existent, your brothers are overprotective, and Mrs. Greene thinks you need glasses because you've been squinting a lot lately. They also think I need to corrupt you. To show you how to have a little fun. They like watching me walk across to your house every night, but they're always disappointed you make me leave so early."

Bayleigh scowled and put her hands on her hips, irritated that the entire neighborhood had been talking about her to Cade. She knew how to have fun. And she had to work a lot if she wanted her store to be a success. There was nothing wrong with that. Unless, of course, you were every person over the age of sixty-five who lived on her street. Apparently they had lots of problems with the way she lived.

"I'm not going to sleep with you just to satisfy all of my geriatric neighbors. That's the lamest thing I've ever heard."

"So what's going on here between us, Bayleigh? We've had fun the last week. We've enjoyed each other's company. And I still want to fuck you so bad I ache with it every second of the day. Are you saying you're not interested?" The half smile on his face was knowing, confident. "Your nipples are hard enough to cut glass."

Bayleigh gasped, offended and turned on at the same time. "Maybe your seduction technique needs a little work. Haven't you ever heard of romance? You think you can just tell me you want to fuck and that'll do it for me? Give me a break."

"Yeah, I think it does do it for you. I bet you're so wet I could slide right into that tight pussy without any foreplay. Some women need romance. You're not one of them, so don't pretend you do. You know your mind and what you like, and you're the least simpering woman I've ever met. When we finally get horizontal we'll meet each other as equals."

"And my seduction technique doesn't need work," he said, stalking her until her back hit the garage wall. "I got you over here, didn't I? Just where I wanted you. And you're not wearing underwear."

"You—you—son of a—"

His fingers covered her lips and his eyes sparkled with laughter. "Don't say anything you'll regret." He braced his hands by both sides of her head, trapping her in his embrace. "Tell me the truth, Bayleigh. Do you want me? I'm too old to play games. We're both adults. There's no reason we can't both get satisfaction and take advantage of where fate has put us. I'm attracted to you, and I want nothing more than to slide between those silky thighs and fuck you until you can't see straight."

"And that's it?" she asked. "A few quick fucks and then we both move on with our lives? Wave friendly hello's as we go into our separate houses and fondly remember a few sweaty nights?"

"More than a few," he said, nuzzling against the sensitive skin on her neck, nipping his way up to her ear where his tongue lightly traced the shell. "My dick's been hard since I laid eyes on you, and I'm tired of jerking off when you're just a few steps away."

Bayleigh gasped as his erotic words slid across her skin like silk. Her nipples brushed against his chest, sending sensations straight to her pussy, and she wanted nothing more than to press into him—to feel the evidence of his arousal.

His lips sipped and teased and he moved his hands from the wall so they skimmed down her body until his fingers bit into the flesh at her hips. He slid them around until they cupped her ass and he pulled her toward him slowly, torturously, until she was begging for contact.

"Please, Cade."

She felt as if all her bones had dissolved into a puddle at his feet. This man had control of her body like no one else ever had. No wonder Paul had called her frigid. She'd been a block of ice compared to what Cade was making her feel now.

"I like hearing my name on your lips." Desire burned in his black eyes, his lids lowered with promise and his nostrils flared at the scent of her arousal. "I know you want me, and I know you think of me. Don't you, Bayleigh?"

His hips anchored hers to the wall and she wrapped her legs around his waist, the hard length of his erection pressing against her. It was too late to hide her arousal from him. She'd never been so wet in her life—her pajama pants soaked through with her need.

"Yessss," she hissed as his fingers slid beneath her shirt and plucked at her nipple. The hand at her ass flexed, and she felt the strength of him in the way his muscles bunched and rippled, even as he held her gently.

"Yes, what?"

His breath feathered against her lips and she could feel the orgasm building inside of her. She shook her head in denial of what was happening to her body. No man had ever brought her so close so quickly. It was as if everything she'd ever known about sex was being turned upside down and inside out.

"I can't, Cade. I can't—"

"Yes you can, baby. Don't ever hide yourself from me. Now answer my question the way I want it answered. Do you think of me fucking you like this?"

"Yes," she screamed as his fingers pinched harder against her nipple. Her body trembled on the brink of fulfillment and her breath heaved in and out of her lungs. She opened her eyes and stared into the black depths of his own, her body and soul overwhelmed by the sheer force of him. "I think of you, Cade. I can't stop thinking about you. Is that what you want to hear?"

"You have no idea how badly I needed to hear that," he whispered against her lips. "You always have to be honest with me. Your body won't deny me the way your mind wants to. I'll always know if you're telling the truth. Don't be scared of this. Just close your eyes and feel."

He didn't give her the choice to do anything *but* feel. He took her mouth in a kiss that put the first they'd shared to shame. Sensations exploded through her body and pleasure rippled across sensitive nerve endings that all seemed to lead to the tight bud hidden between her folds. His hands slipped beneath the elastic waist of her pajama pants, and colors danced behind her closed lids at the intimate touch.

"Sweet Jesus," he panted, his fingers finding the bare flesh, feeling the proof of her desire. "I'm going to taste you, Bayleigh. Lap up every bit of that sweet cream that's drenching my fingers. Do you know how I've wanted you for the past two weeks, driving myself crazy, imagining it was me fucking you instead of that damned vibrator you use?"

She stiffened in his arms, mortification filling her soul even as the blood rushed to her cheeks from forbidden desire. Her head dropped to his shoulder and mewls of pleasure escaped her throat from the sensations rioting through her body, even as she tried to push him away.

"Don't get all tense on me now, sugar. You think I didn't know what you were doing in that bed? Why do you think I spent so much time on my deck? You'd push me out the door, so turned on I could all but feel the sparks against my skin, and then you'd go in your room and turn all the lights out and pleasure yourself with that fucking piece of rubber when it should have be me. I could hear you call my name every time you came."

She breathed in sharply as his fingers slid inside her in one smooth stroke, stretching her and driving her crazy at the same time, so the pleasure-pain brought her right to the edge. All thoughts of embarrassment disappeared and desperation filled her.

"I need you inside me, Cade. I'm begging you."

"We'll get there, sweetheart," he promised. "Listening to you come night after night made my cock so hard I thought I would explode from wanting you. Did you ever watch me from your bed? Could you see me unzip my jeans and wrap my fingers around my dick? Did you watch me stroke it until I came all over my hand?"

"No," Bayleigh cried, wishing she'd known to watch

him.

The thought of him taking himself that way while she was lying in bed only a short distance away had her itching to make the visions in her mind a reality.

"There's no need to deny the desire between us, but I'm not looking for anything serious here. I'll always be honest with you, just as you will be with me. Can you go through with this, Bayleigh? I know you're not the type of woman to have casual flings."

"Then why are you doing this to me?" she cried out as he added a third finger, his thumb rubbing in gentle circles around the taut bud of her clit.

"Because you want it. Just as much as I do. And sometimes you just need to stop thinking about the future and enjoy what's right in front of you. Can you live with what I'm offering?"

She opened her eyes and saw the stark lines of passion on his face, the determination in his eyes for her to agree to whatever he demanded from her. But hidden beneath the determination was the sheen of vulnerability—of a past that was too painful to bear.

"I don't know," she finally said.

But her denial was like fighting a losing battle. She didn't have the strength to be around him and not want him. The only thing she could hope for was that her heart wouldn't be too scarred when he decided to walk away.

"Do you want me to stop?" he asked, arching a brow, a

smug smile on his face as he brought her closer to orgasm.

It was impossible to think with him tormenting parts of her body that hadn't been touched by a man for almost three years. Could she do what he was asking? She wasn't the type to go to bed with a man just for the hell of it. She'd never had a one night stand, and it had been weeks into her other relationships before she'd agreed to go to take the next step. Of course, look how that turned out. All of her lovers had been disappointed anyway.

His fingers curled inside her and her eyes rolled back into her head as new sensations assaulted her battered system. Desire like this couldn't possibly last. They'd end up killing each other. Maybe the best thing to do would be to get it out of her system. Just so she could function on a normal level again.

"Answer me, Bayleigh." His voice was rough and his drawl slurred with passion.

"I need to come, Cade," she begged. "Please let me come."

"Yeah, baby," he groaned, taking her lips in another hot kiss. "I want you to come all over my fingers. All you need to do is answer me."

"Yes!" The scream tore from the pit of her stomach. "I don't care about anything else. Just fuck me."

"Good girl," he groaned. "I need to be inside you, Bayleigh. I've never needed anything so much." He withdrew his fingers, drinking in her disappointed cries with a gentleness she wasn't expecting. "Just a minute, baby. I can't fuck you out here. I'm sure the neighbors have gotten more of a show than we needed to give them as it is."

Bayleigh tightened her legs around him as he made love to her mouth with slow, sliding thrusts of his tongue, and her finger tangled in the length of his hair, reveling at the silky softness. She sucked at his tongue and ground her pussy against the denim of his jeans, so close to an orgasm she thought she'd probably lose it by the time he finally got inside of her. The only time she'd ever been remotely close to orgasming with one of her previous lovers, he'd changed positions and the feeling had evaporated like mist.

Frustration clouded her cries as Cade stumbled toward the door that led inside his house. He cursed as stacks of boxes got in the way, and he finally set her down on a dining room table she hoped like hell was sturdy enough to hold their weight.

Cade unwound her legs from around his waist and stripped the pajama pants off her legs, her panties following, so she was completely bare to him from the waist down.

"Christ, Bayleigh," he panted. "Look how pretty you are." He trailed a finger across her stomach to the bare folds between her legs, slicked with her desire for him. "I love that you're bare for me. I'll be able to taste every inch of you, and you'll be able to feel me completely."

"Cade!" she screamed as his long fingers slid inside her once again.

There wasn't time to prepare or think about the sensations bombarding her body. The thoughts that usually plagued her at moments like this were absent—her wondering if her lover was disappointed in her, or if she'd be able to come. There wasn't room for thought with Cade overwhelming all of her senses at once.

He lifted her shirt so it rested just above her breasts and groaned as he bent forward to taste them.

"Oh, baby," he said, licking her nipple with the flat of his tongue. "You have the sexiest tits. Full and lush, with nipples like little raspberries. And they taste just as sweet."

Her breasts were swollen and aching, and he sucked her nipple with enough pressure that she could feel every pull throbbing in her clit. Her eyes rolled back and her lids fluttered closed as the force of his suction grew, his tongue flicking across her rigid nipple, and his finger moving in slow, steady thrusts in her vagina.

The spasms seemed to come from everyone and nowhere all at once, her body jerking against him with uncontrollable strength, and she begged him to stop even as she prayed for him to continue. The sensations were more than she could handle, and she exploded against him in a symphony of light and color, screaming his name as shudders rocked her body.

"Fuck, that's hot," Cade whispered, kissing his way from her breast back to her lips. "My hand is soaked with your come. Do you know what it does to me to know you wanted me that much?"

Bayleigh's body shook with tremors, and she didn't have the strength to do anything more than lift her eyelids a fraction of an inch. She watched him straighten and unfasten the button of his jeans, the rigid length of his cock causing her to gasp in admiration and horror. All she could think was that she hadn't bought a big enough vibrator.

Chimes echoed in her head, and it wasn't until she heard his muttered curses that she realized the sound came from the phone that sat on the butcher block island in the center of his kitchen.

"Shit," he growled. "I have to get that. It's the station."

The transformation in him was amazing. His eyes went from melted dark chocolate to cold fire in an instant, and he left her open and exposed on the table as he stalked to the phone, his body under rigid control.

"MacKenzie," he barked into the phone.

Bayleigh closed her eyes in mortification. She'd never lost control like that before. There wasn't a hole deep enough for her to crawl in. As if her lack of control wasn't bad enough, she could feel the wetness from her orgasm cooling beneath her bottom. *That* had certainly never happened before either. And she hoped to God it never happened again.

Relocating was the only way to get past this. She'd never lived in Alaska. Or maybe she should be thinking abroad.

"Where did you find her?" she heard Cade ask.

There was no way she was going to be able to face him again today. Not after losing herself to him like that. She found the strength to slide off the table, surprised her legs were able to hold her upright, and she ignored his narrowed eyes as she picked up her pajama pants off the floor and slipped them on. She pulled her shirt down so her breasts were covered, and smoothed her hair down nervously.

"Fine," Cade finally said to whoever was on the other end of the line. "I'm on my way now. See if the ME will wait to take her until I can get there."

Bayleigh had the door that led back into the garage open and one foot out the door when she heard him toss the phone back on the counter.

"Where the hell are you going?" He moved quickly and silently, and he was so close she could feel his breath on the back of her neck.

"You obviously have to leave," she said, refusing to turn around and meet his eyes. "I've got things to do today, so I thought I'd head back home."

"Don't think for one second that this is over between us, Bayleigh. I saw the look on your face when you came. You have nothing to be embarrassed about, and I want you so fucking bad my balls are aching with it."

She let him turn her around and into his arms, and damned if her body didn't betray her with just one touch. She arched against him like a cat as his hands ran down her back.

"I don't know if I can do this after all, Cade. It might be too much for me to handle. I'm not used to—this," she said lamely, encompassing them both with her hands. "It's very intense."

"Then you've been missing out, sugar. And what we have is hot as hell. That asshole you were engaged to obviously didn't know a clit from a bellybutton. Don't try to run from me. Just hang on and enjoy the ride."

She looked at him solemnly, the magnitude of the promise she'd made to him weighing down on her. There was no way she could give her body to this man as completely as she just had and not give him her heart as well. Cade MacKenzie had the power to do what Paul hadn't. Paul had whittled away at her self-esteem until it was in shreds, but Cade had the ability to destroy her soul. There was no way she could let that happen.

"You've got a job to do," she said, kissing him lightly on the cheek in farewell. "I'll see you around."

She headed out through the garage, but she stopped when she heard him call her name. The urge to go back into his arms was so strong it made her want to weep, but she kept her back turned and her steps determined.

"I'll be back tonight, Bayleigh. We're going to talk about this."

"I'm busy tonight," she lied. "Goodbye, Cade. Be careful."

The trip back to her house seemed impossibly long. She knew Mrs. Spillers across the street was looking out her kitchen window and that Mr. Krentz was pretending to trim his hedges as he watched her walk to her front door, but she couldn't think about her behavior yet. There was no way her brothers wouldn't find out what she'd been doing in Cade's garage, but that was a problem for another time.

Her eyes stung with unshed tears as she closed her front door behind her. A man like Cade MacKenzie wasn't in the cards for her. He was too hard, too demanding, and he'd never let her get away with giving him anything but all she had to offer.

She wasn't willing to sacrifice everything for a casual fuck buddy. That wasn't her, and she'd let him convince her she'd be all right with the non-intimacy of a real relationship. But she had dreams of a family and a man who loved her. She might have been engaged to the wrong man before, but at least she was trying to find happiness. Cade had just given up on it.

There was no way she could stay cooped up in the house today. And she sure as hell didn't want to face him when he got home from wherever he was going. She'd just have to avoid him. His late night visits and the constant temptation he presented would have to stop.

It sounded good in theory. Now all she had to do was convince her body to do as her mind wanted.

CHAPTER SEVEN

Fluorescent lights flickered in an unhealthy shade of green over Cade's desk, casting ghoulish shadows over the case file he'd been poring over for the last hour. He'd spent all day at the crime scene, making himself as large a target as possible.

It wouldn't be long before the cartel made contact. At least, he'd thought it wouldn't be long. Maybe his instincts were off after all. He'd been in town two weeks, and they hadn't done anything but send him messages through the women they'd decided to use the drug on. There were three bodies on his conscience now. If the cartel didn't make a move soon he was going to have to do something to draw them out.

He'd delayed going home as long as he could—at the crime scene and now at the station—but the cartel still hadn't made contact. He was sure it would have been today.

Warm air ruffled the papers on his desk as the heater

kicked on, only heightening the smell of stale coffee and sweat. He finished typing up the report from the crime scene and shook his head at the cruelty of these men. He'd never understood it, but he accepted it—to the point that he was always surprised when someone did something good instead of the other way around. There were no rose colored glasses left in his life.

The rundown bar just off Avenue P and 15th Street didn't fit the profile of where a drug like *Rabbit* was used. The clientele who could afford the drug weren't known to frequent seedier places to get their fix—where the booze was cheap and the women cheaper. They didn't want their victims used up and rough. They wanted fresh-faced girls from good families. Girls who had a future. Girls they could destroy. It only added to the high when they raped them.

So Cade's instincts started humming the moment he'd gotten the call about another murder—the only difference between this one and the other victims being that the deceased was a prostitute. He'd made the forty-five minute trip to the other side of town to the crime scene, when he'd had the sudden urge to turn the truck around and head back to Bayleigh. Something wasn't right, but damned if he knew which direction to head until he could get tangible proof of where they were watching him from. He hadn't felt eyes on his house, but that didn't mean they didn't have them there.

The top men in del Fuego's cartel had been as well trained as any soldiers or agents he'd worked with. Hell, he'd helped train some of them during his time there. If they didn't want him to know they were there, then he wouldn't know plain and simple. All he could go by was the instincts that had been ingrained into him over the last sixteen years.

And those instincts hadn't failed him as his truck pulled up to the crime scene. He'd felt the crosshairs on the back of his head from the moment he'd stepped onto the graveled pavement. But only because they'd wanted him to know they were there. They wouldn't take him out so soon.

The victim had been brutally raped and strangled. The syringe in her arm filled with the drug was just overkill, as she'd already been dead by the time it had been given to her. No one would waste a quarter of a million dollar drug on a prostitute unless they were trying to send him a message.

And it had been one hell of a message. Cade's name had been carved into her thigh just below the number three, signifying she was the third victim. The cartel was sending him a message that they were out for blood. His in particular.

The cartel was playing a game he didn't want to be caught in the middle of. They didn't care who got caught in the crossfire, which meant he had to shut them down before more bodies started piling up. Three in the two weeks he'd been in town was three too many.

He closed the file he'd been staring at blankly and locked it in his desk drawer. Thoughts of Bayleigh had been bombarding him all day—visions of her laid out on the table, drenching his fingers, and so fucking hot he'd almost come in his jeans. She was distracting him, stirring up thoughts he hadn't had in a long time, and she was making it damned hard to keep his attention on his job. He was here to draw out the remaining cartel members. Period. Not to fuck his neighbor. And certainly not to get attached to her, or let those emotions he'd thought were destroyed after Carmen's death come to the surface again. But damned if he could help himself.

The station was all but empty except for a few uniform cops coming in early for third shift. He grabbed his leather jacket from the back of his chair and was just slipping it on when his cell phone rang. The number was blocked and he knew this was the contact he'd been waiting for. Someone at the DEA would be monitoring the call and they'd be trying to run a trace, but they wouldn't find the source that easily.

"MacKenzie," he answered.

"Long time no see, *cabron*." The voice was lightly accented and familiar. That of a petulant child who'd grown up with a monster for a father and every creature comfort at his fingertips. It had always amazed him the Carlos and Carmen were related.

"I heard you've decided to be a city cop," Carlos said, the sneer evident. Local cops had been easy to buy off in Miami. It was part of the reason the DEA had had such a difficult time pinning down the cartel members. "Tell me it ain't so. It seems like such a waste of talent."

"I didn't realize you cared, Carlos. I would have forwarded you my address had I known you were looking for me."

Cade made his way to the bank of windows that overlooked the street and opened the blinds a quarter turn. Headlights cut into the darkness and a few pedestrians walked along the sidewalks, headed into the restaurant across the street. But it was sparsely populated. There was no sign of Carlos that he could see.

"Don't think for a second that I haven't always known where you were, asshole. You think I would just forget about what you did to Carmen?"

Cade's gut clenched and he closed his eyes as memories assaulted him, but he forced his voice to stay light and uncaring. "You've got a faulty memory, Carlos. You see, I remember your father putting that bullet through her brain. So how is that my fault again?"

The breathing on the other end of the line grew heavy with rage and Cade smiled. Carlos had never had the control his father did, which was why they'd have a much better shot at taking down the cartel with Carlos behind the wheel. Cade closed the blinds and slipped down the back stairs, jogging down the three flights to the gated parking lot behind the precinct.

"Listen closely, MacKenzie," Carlos said. "Because your days are numbered. Did you know the only reason you're alive is because my father gave the order that you're not to be touched?"

Cade raised his eyebrows in surprise at that bit of information. "What can I say? Miguel always did like me best."

"And look what it got him. Serves him right, if you ask me."

Cade shook his head. He didn't understand families like

the del Fuego's—flesh and blood who would murder you instead of stand beside you, betray you for a bigger piece of the pie. His family might be a little overwhelming and wouldn't hesitate to butt into your business without asking, but they'd stand beside you when times were tough, and they'd fight like hell to protect you if you were in trouble.

Carlos' voice was laced with pain and bitterness. "Father said he needed you alive because it would drive you crazy not being able to kill him. That not knowing when and how the cartel would strike would possess you until you became careless. You think you destroyed my legacy by having your American soldiers and agents come down on my family? Homeland Security thought they could capture my father and use his knowledge to their benefit, but he outsmarted them. He's been running the cartel right under their noses."

Cade opened the door leading to the parking lot, and pressed the button on his key chain to start his truck. The engine caught immediately, and he breathed a sigh of relief. The last thing he needed was to find himself splattered in a million different pieces across the pavement. The cartel was fond of using explosives to do their dirty work when up close and personal couldn't be accomplished.

"This is all very fascinating, Carlos. But you forget, I was there when Miguel was arrested and taken in. The cartel is in pieces and your father is in lockdown. And you're starting to bore me. The last I heard, you didn't have the balls to go against dear old dad. So why are you here?"

"I'm here for you," Carlos said with a sneer. "I guess your friends at DHS didn't pass on the news. Miguel is in a coma. Seems like someone snuck in some bad shit and gave him a taste of his own medicine."

Fuck, Cade thought. Someone should have told him. If Miguel wasn't in charge of the struggling cartel then someone else would be. It was always better the devil you know.

"Speechless, MacKenzie? Things aren't looking good for the old man. Lucky for me. Not so lucky for you. The cartel is now completely under my control. And I don't care how much Miguel wants you alive. The orders are mine to give now. And we've been watching you these last weeks, planning for your arrival."

"So come get me," Cade taunted. "You think I haven't felt your eyes on me? I've been waiting on you, Carlos. What's taken so long?"

Harsh laughter assaulted his ears and he checked his rearview mirror as he pulled out into traffic. He immediately saw the black sedan pull in behind him, not even bothering to be subtle about following. Cade recognized the guy driving the car. He'd been a lower level soldier in the cartel when Cade had been there, but it looked as if he'd worked his way up in the world.

"You always were a cocky bastard, MacKenzie."

"But it was me your father was going to hand the cartel to instead of his own son. Why do you think that was, Carlos?"

Cade felt the waves of anger pulsing through the phone and kept his eye on the car tailing him, testing how serious the situation was by taking a couple of side streets and cutting off a couple of cars to take a quick exit. The guy stayed on his ass like white on rice.

"Because my father was weak, and he couldn't see a liar when he was standing right in front of his face. I never liked you," Carlos spat out. "And I knew you weren't what you seemed. Now you'll pay for Carmen's death and for destroying what should have rightfully been mine. The cartel isn't what it once was, but I still have product and I still have loyal men. Don't underestimate me."

"I'd never dream of it," Cade said. "What do you want, Carlos? If you think I'm going to make this easy on you, you've got another thing coming."

"Oh, no. It's you who have had it much too easy. What good would it do to kill you if you didn't suffer first? When was the last time you talked to your sister?" he asked. "I spoke to her myself just last week. She seems to be doing quite well. Finishing up her Master's Degree and living in that big house all by herself while her brothers are out saving the world and her parents are doing a little traveling in their retirement years. You should take better care of what's yours."

A cold chill slid down Cade's spine and terror gripped his heart. They'd taught Darcy how to protect herself, but she was no match against Carlos or one of his men. She was also head-strong and impulsive, which had gotten her into trouble more times than it had gotten her out of it.

"Where is she?" Cade bit out, terrified he'd be too late.

"Oh, she's safe and sound, tucked into bed, my friend. At least for now. But she's turned into a beautiful young woman. All that silky black hair and those violet eyes. Should I fuck her first before I kill her like you did my sister?"

"Stay away from her," Cade bit out. "I will hunt you down for this, Carlos. You have no idea what I'm capable of."

"I think I do. But I believe in an eye for an eye, and I don't see why you should have your sister when you've deprived me of my own. It hardly seems fair."

The urge to hang up and call home was prevalent in his mind, but he held on, knowing that's exactly what Carlos would expect him to do.

"You know, MacKenzie, I've never understood your appeal to the opposite sex. You hadn't been in the compound three days before Carmen spread her legs for you. Fucking *puta.* She'd been a good girl before you came along."

Cade still remembered his surprise as he'd broken through the barrier of Carmen's virginity. She'd responded to his touch unlike any virgin he'd ever known, not that he'd had a lot of experience with virgins, but it had caused him to stop and reevaluate the woman he thought he'd understood. She'd been everything good and innocent in the world—everything the rest of her family could never hope to be—and he'd taken a part of that innocence from her because it had been part of the plan. He hadn't loved her until much later, and that guilt still ate at him.

"That's a hell of a way to talk about your own sister, Carlos. Maybe you should get therapy to release all that hostility. It can't be good for you."

Carlos ignored his taunt, his anger already fueling the fire. "History has a way of repeating itself, *Si*? I enjoyed the little scene you and the whore next door put on for me and my men this morning. They were horny as hell after you left, leaving her there all alone while you went to look at the message I'd left you. You can see right through those flimsy lace curtains she has up. And she makes sure to raise the blinds back up after you leave every night. What's with that, Cade? You don't want us to see you screwing your new whore? When did you become shy?"

"Fuck you, Carlos. Stay away from Bayleigh."

"It's too late for that. You marked her as yours. I hope that brings her comfort when I rub the drug across her silky skin and let my men have her."

The sigh on the other end of the line had Cade's anger escalating to the point that he could feel his control disappearing. He knew what men saw when they looked at Bayleigh.

"Her body is something else, my man. Fine tits and ass, and a mouth that's going to suck me dry before she takes her last breath. Just the thought is enough to get me off."

Cade growled low in his throat and he was barely able to choke the words out. "I'm coming for you, Carlos."

Carlos laughed. "You've got to find me first."

Cade disconnected the phone and pushed the pedal all the way to the floor, and he noticed the car tailing him stayed close long enough to wave at him and take the next exit. Which meant they had men set up to watch him at the house. *Shit.*

He used the Bluetooth system in his truck to call in a favor. He couldn't be in two places at one time, and he needed someone to watch over Darcy. To make sure she was safe. There was only one man he could call—one man he trusted with his life—to make sure she didn't get into trouble.

The only problem was that the man in question was Bayleigh's oldest brother. There was no way he could tell Brant about his involvement with Bayleigh or that Bayleigh was in danger—though there was a chance the DHS agent already knew. Cade needed Brant to protect Darcy and not ask questions.

Fortunately, Brant owed him a hell of a favor since Cade had taken a bullet for his friend a couple of years ago. The angle of the shot would have meant Brant's death, and Cade knew he could survive if he intercepted it. The short of it was: Brant Scott owed him a hell of a favor, and he was about to collect.

"What?" Brant said on the other end of the line.

"I need help, and I don't need questions," Cade said quickly. "I'm running out of time."

There was a slight pause before Brant said, "Done."

"Protect Darcy. Carlos del Fuego has put out a hit on

her. It might already be too late."

"I've got her covered," Brant said. "I got the word this morning about the change of power in the cartel. It seems some asshole at DHS was hoping the news of Miguel's coma wouldn't become public knowledge, so they've been sitting on it for three weeks. Heads will roll by the time I'm through with them."

Cade believed it. Brant was a Special Agent in Charge for DHS, and he wasn't without power. In fact, he always wondered if Brant was higher up on the food chain than even he knew.

"As long as Darcy is safe," Cade said.

"I've got my sights on your house as we speak. I knew they'd be after her. I let your cousin, Cooper, know about the danger. I figured he'd be pissed if he didn't know something could go down since he's the sheriff."

"That's an understatement." Cooper would have agents for breakfast and spit them out if he found out something was going on in his town and no one had informed him.

Brant grunted in agreement. "Coop's going to keep an eye on Grant and his wife so I don't have to split my attention. I figured the threat to Darcy was the biggest since she's by herself and basically unprotected."

Cade let out a slow breath, grateful his friend had a sixth sense about these kinds of things. No one was more important than his family, and their safety was first priority. Knowing his brother and sister were being watched after was a hell of a relief. And knowing Shane was out of the country on his own mission meant that he wouldn't step into the middle of things for at least another few weeks. By then, he was hoping it would all be over. The only wild card was Declan. It was impossible to outguess him.

"I want you inside the house," Cade said. "I don't care how big of a fit she throws. I want you to be her shadow until the threat is gone. Tell her I've given you permission to jerk her into a safe house if she doesn't cooperate."

The sigh on the other end of the line would have made him laugh at any other time, because Darcy was a handful and everybody who'd ever spent five minutes in her company knew it. But the panic entrenched inside him was too deep, too clawing, and the need to get to Bayleigh pressed in on him until his chest felt like it was being crushed by cinder blocks. He sped in and out of traffic, hoping like hell he wasn't too late to save her. The thought of anything happening to her was terrifying, and it brought back thoughts and feelings he'd buried a long time ago.

"I'll owe you," Cade said.

"We're even, my friend. Keep Bayleigh safe," he said. "And don't do anything that will make me have to kill you later."

Brant disconnected and Cade shook his head. Bayleigh would be pissed if she found out her brother was having her watched. It was the only way he would have known that Cade had inserted himself neatly into her life on such short notice.

He checked the rearview mirror again and didn't see

another tail, so he turned the truck onto a well-trafficked side street and left it parked there. He sent a quick text to Declan and put his phone in his back pocket. There was enough moon out to see once his eyes adjusted to the darkness, but not enough that he couldn't hide himself in the shadows.

It was a half-mile hike through the treed area behind his house, and he was grateful there hadn't been much rain lately so the creek was running low. His .9mm rested comfortably in his hand, and he blended in with the darkness as he came up on the back of his house. The lamps he'd left on in his living room glowed softly through the shades he'd pulled down before he left, but it wasn't his house that had the hairs at the back of his neck standing on end.

Bayleigh's house was cast in complete darkness. In the two weeks he'd been there, she consistently left her back porch light on and a couple of lamps switched on throughout the house. She also left the light over her kitchen sink on all the time. The house was *never* in complete darkness.

He edged out of the trees and into the open expanse of her backyard, his footsteps silent as he approached the open deck and arbor area. The tiniest sound to his left had him stopping, his ears pricked for the familiar sounds of the enemy. Unless they were trained as he had been, it was hard for a person to stay completely still for long periods of time.

Carlos was playing a game, stringing him along until he was ready to move in for the kill. And he'd made Bayleigh a player, just because Cade had been too hot for her to keep his hands to himself. If Bayleigh was in the game, then he had no choice but to keep her close to him. For her own protection.

The sound came again and he had his gun pointed with his finger on the trigger before the target had the chance to duck for cover.

"Don't move one fucking muscle," he growled.

CHAPTER EIGHT

Bayleigh gasped as the dull sheen of the gun glinted in the moonlight, and she sunk to her chin in the hot tub, feeling a little too exposed in the tiny black bikini she wore. All she'd wanted was to soak away the day in peace and quiet, and neither of those words were ones she'd use in conjunction with Cade MacKenzie. She'd thought turning out all the lights and pretending like she wasn't home would discourage him from seeking her out. She just needed time. But clearly her plan had failed.

After he'd left her earlier that morning, she'd done nothing but think about his touch all day, as if she were an addict waiting for her next fix. She'd never climaxed like that before—never even thought it possible to lose such complete control of mind and body. It was disturbing and arousing at the same time.

Cade had managed to strip away the layers she'd built over the last several years in a matter of minutes. If she was being honest with herself, he'd gotten to her in the first five minutes after they'd met.

That was her problem. Her pattern. She believed in the possibility of soulmates, in the happily-ever-after. And because of her childhood and the instability she'd had by not having a permanent home, she was constantly looking for the one person who could give her that happily-ever-after and the stability she craved.

Those thoughts had been swirling around her mind like the water cocooning her body when she'd felt another presence close by. She couldn't hear or see anyone, but she definitely felt them. Her brothers had always told her to trust her first instinct because it was usually right. She hadn't thought she'd made any noise, but screaming for help or running for cover was out of the question by the time she saw the weapon pointed in her direction. He'd been that silent. That quick. And obviously that deadly.

"Don't move one fucking muscle," Cade said, his voice barely carrying across the small distance between them. "Have you lost your mind, Bayleigh? What the hell are you doing out here?"

Bayleigh swallowed nervously. Seeing him this way was disconcerting. He moved like the night itself, his body lithe and graceful like a cat stalking its prey, and his face was hard—his eyes lethal. This was a man who could kill without blinking an eye.

"The last I checked this was my property and I didn't have to check in with you to relax," she said, annoyed at the way she'd cowered. "Thanks for blowing that all to hell, by the way."

"I thought you were in trouble," he said between gritted teeth. "All the lights are off in your house and you have absolutely zero protection out here if someone wanted to hurt you."

Bayleigh felt the heat rush to her cheeks and she damned her tongue even as she opened her mouth. "The lights are out in my house because I wanted you to get a clue. I didn't feel like dealing with you again today. And I knew you were in my yard the moment you stepped onto my property."

"Yeah?" he asked. He turned so the moonlight glinted off the whites of his narrowed eyes. He didn't look happy. "If I'd been the enemy, you knowing I was here wouldn't have done you a lot of good. You would have been too late to take cover. Meaning you'd be dead."

"This isn't Baghdad, Cade. What enemies? I have no enemies? You, on the other hand, probably have more than you know what to do with. Don't you think you're overreacting just a little bit?"

She heard the slide of metal against leather as he holstered his weapon and breathed a sigh of relief. Her dad and brothers had made sure she knew how to shoot a gun, but she'd never been comfortable with them. And she found she especially didn't like having one pointed at her.

"No, I'm not overreacting," he said, running a frustrated hand through his hair. "Come on. We need to talk." He held out the towel to her, but she was already shaking her head no.

"I meant what I said this morning, Cade." She ignored his outstretched hand and relaxed back down in the water, closing her eyes as if that would suddenly make him disappear. "You're sexy as hell and we obviously have some chemistry, but I'm not cut out for this. I know what I want and need in a man, and you're not it. I can't do meaningless fucks. I'm just not built that way. So just give me some space and go home."

Bayleigh didn't even feel him coming until it was too late. She squeaked as he pulled her out of the water and wrapped the towel around her with perfunctory movements. Her arms were trapped in the towel, so she couldn't fight as he tossed her over his shoulder like a bag of potatoes and walked across her backyard to his house.

"Not one sound, Bayleigh, or I'm going to spank your ass so red you won't be able to sit down for a week."

She froze against him, her pussy clenching at the thought of his hand against her bare bottom. Jesus, this man was dangerous to every shred of sanity left in her head. The thought of being spanked had always been a turnoff. Or so she'd thought. But as soon as the words came out of his mouth, she was gushing like a waterfall in anticipation.

He unlocked his back door and pushed it open, the cool air escaping and bringing chills to her skin. Bayleigh bit her lip as he pulled his weapon from the holster and nudged the door open a little further with his foot. Once they were inside and the door was closed he set her on her feet and took her chin between his finger and thumb.

"Stay right here until I get back," he said, and the look in his eyes told her if she disobeyed she wasn't going to like the consequences. She nodded and took a step back as he made his way through the house, checking the alarm system and inside all the closets.

She hadn't seen this part of his house when she'd been inside earlier that morning, not that she'd really been paying attention to any part of the house with his tongue down her throat and his fingers shoved inside her. But now that she had the opportunity to look around, she found the inside of Cade's home an interesting study of the man himself. It was cozy—masculine.

A few boxes were still stacked against the wall, but all of the furniture was arranged—a worn brown leather couch that look comfortable for napping and a hooked rug in neutral colors sat in the middle of the floor. The tables were old and heavy, and a couple of overstuffed chairs flanked the fireplace. It was a comfortable room, and made Cade seem a hell of a lot more human than when she'd first laid eyes on him.

By the time he finally came back from checking the house, she was shivering in earnest and worry began to penetrate the fog of lust that seemed to surround her whenever he was near. He was acting awfully strange.

"What's going on, Cade?"

He unhooked his shoulder holster and put it in the top drawer of the buffet he had in his dining room, and her mouth went dry as he stripped his t-shirt over his head and tossed it onto the couch, not bothering to answer her question. He came toward her with purpose, and her hand clenched the towel she'd tightened around her breasts.

"We're going to finish what we started this morning," he said. "I'm going to sink inside that sweet pussy until I can think again, because I swear I haven't been able to get you out of my head since you threw those keys at my head. And after we've fucked ourselves into near exhaustion, we're going to have a conversation about what's going on."

Bayleigh put a hand against his chest to ward him off, but it was difficult keeping her attention on the task with the feel of his muscles taut beneath her fingertips. He was hot to the touch, the hair on his chest just an added texture of sensation.

"I'm not stupid, Cade, and you're not going to distract me by taking me to bed. I've already told you I changed my mind, though I'd be happy to play Monopoly if you're just lonely."

She almost smiled at the way his eyes narrowed. The man didn't like to be told no, and she enjoyed the way his temper frayed around the edges and the veins in his neck pulsed whenever she stood up to him.

"Tell me what's going on," she said. "Are you in trouble? Is it the case you're working? My brother said—" Bayleigh clamped her mouth shut, but it was too late. The damage had been done.

"Your brother said what?" he asked.

His eyes darkened and she tried not to flinch as he reached for her. She wasn't expecting the gentle caress of his fingers against the back of her hand, and she felt guilty for thinking the worst. Violence lived inside Cade, no doubt, but she knew to her soul that he was a good man. She'd seen it when he'd mentioned his family—the love and affection that gleamed in his eyes. And her own brother respected Cade, she'd been able to tell by the way he talked about him.

She let out a long, slow breath as he took her wrist and brought her hand to his chest, all the while moving closer until she was trapped between his hard body and the back of his couch.

"Have you been checking up on me, Bayleigh?"

"No, not on purpose. But that doesn't mean my brothers won't stop from offering their opinions whether I want them or not. Brady still hasn't learned to mind his own business. Brant's only marginally better."

"And I guess you're not very good at taking their advice, otherwise you wouldn't have been in my garage this morning coming around my fingers."

"Stop trying to distract me from my question, dammit." She pushed against him but he didn't budge, and the erection growing against her stomach was beginning to become a distraction. "Brady also said you were working a case with the DEA. Is that why you were sneaking through my backyard like a thief?"

"I like a woman who's determined to get what she wants," his smile was sharp and she saw a flash of straight white teeth just before he nipped at her bottom lip. "It just makes it that much more satisfying when I have her begging beneath me."

"I'm not going to give up," she warned.

"God, I hope not."

He loosened the towel she was clutching to her chest, and her breath caught as his fingers traced of the swell of her breasts. Her breasts were so sensitive, every stroke vibrating through her pussy as if he were already touching her there.

Bayleigh's thoughts scattered as he took her mouth in a hot kiss, his tongue sliding inside and warring with her own. She couldn't push him away. Not again. At least not until she'd had him inside her. It seemed as if she'd been waiting for ages, and she couldn't deny herself any longer.

He tugged at the string of her bikini top and she felt the cups loosen—the only thing holding the damp fabric in place was his chest pressed against hers. His hands glided down her back and cupped her ass, pulling her against his erection, and she hooked one leg around his waist to try and maximize the pleasure.

"There's no stopping this time, Bayleigh. I'm going to take you every way I can. I'll invade your body and mind to the point that everything you do will make you think of me—will make you want me more."

His mouth found hers again, almost frantically, and he circled her into the bedroom, her senses so clouded with lust she went dizzy with the sensation. His thumbs hooked in her bathing suit bottoms and he pulled them down so they fell around her ankles. She cried out when she felt his fingers skim down her back and into the drenched folds between her legs. He sank two fingers into the soaking depths of her pussy and pulled them back out, repeating the motion over and over again until her knees gave out and his arm tightened around her waist to keep her from collapsing.

Her back arched and his head came down, his mouth clamping around her nipple and his teeth scraping against the sensitive bud. His fingers gathered the moisture from her vagina and trailed to the tiny puckered hole of her anus, circling the forbidden entrance.

"Cade," she panted, shaking her head as his finger pressed into the tight passage.

"You're hungry for me here," he whispered, gathering more moisture from her pussy and bringing it back to her rear passage, this time pushing two fingers inside her. "You're squeezing my fingers as if you don't want to let me go. You'll do the same to my cock, tightening around it as I fuck you with long, slow strokes."

"No, Cade. I can't," she whimpered. "It's too much."

He repeated the motions, gathering moisture and lubricating her back hole, over and over again until she was pushing against him, eager for his penetration. And when his mouth surrounded her nipple once more and began to suck it in time to the rhythm of his fingers, she was lost.

She came undone. Her ass clenched around his fingers and her pussy released the juices of her desire. Silent screams echoed in her mind as she shattered into a million pieces and darkness covered her like a blanket. Time and space ceased to exist.

Bayleigh sighed as cool sheets touched her back and Cade's lips whispered across her skin like butterfly kisses. She was floating in weightless bliss. But it wasn't until she felt the cool metal of cuffs latch around her wrists that her eyes popped open. A lone candle flickered from the nightstand, but it was enough light for her to see her surroundings.

She didn't remember him taking the time to light a candle. *Jesus, how long had she been out?*

The huge bed she laid on dominated the center of the room—massive columns spearing up from the four corners—and the cuffs were attached to a long piece of black rope so her arms were raised straight above her head.

"What the hell, Cade?" She rattled the cuffs, pulled at the rope, but there was no give as she tugged.

"I told you I was going to tie you to my bed."

He stood by the side of the bed and undid the button of his jeans. His arousal was thick and hard behind the denim, and her breath caught at the memory of how he'd looked the last time she'd seen him—impossibly huge. But greed warred with the worry.

"Remember that first day, Bayleigh? As soon as I mentioned my handcuffs your nipples tightened and the pulse in your neck fluttered."

He pushed his jeans past his hips and stepped out of them, letting her look her fill. Her mouth watered at the sight of him. The man should never wear clothes. His chest and abs rippled with muscles, and the little indentions just above each side of his pelvic bone had her licking her lips with the need to bite him just there. He had another tattoo she hadn't noticed low on his stomach, a smaller design similar to the one that wrapped around his shoulder and down his arm.

She'd noticed the scar on his right hand and the jagged white marks on his chest, but the puckered tissue along his thigh brought tears to her eyes. How had he survived the wounds that marred his body? They didn't repulse her at all—only added to his overall appeal—but they did make her wonder who he really was. The life he'd led.

"I wish you could see the look in your eyes," he said, crawling on the bed beside her.

She struggled against the bonds again, wanting nothing more than to be able to touch him. "I don't like this, Cade. I want to be able to touch you. I won't be controlled by any man."

"You'll get your chance, sweetheart. In fact, I'm going to make sure that you get to touch me. I've dreamed of that sexy mouth of yours taking my cock, swallowing me whole."

Bayleigh licked her lips nervously as he came closer, pushing pillows beneath her head so she was propped at a good angle. He ran his fingers through her hair and straddled her, so his cock was lined up with her lips.

"Take me, Bayleigh. Let me fuck your mouth."

The drop of pre-cum that glistened at the end of his cock was too much temptation, and her tongue flicked out, tasting the salty essence that burst against her tongue.

"Fuck," he growled, his head dropping back on his shoulders.

Her mouth opened around him and her tongue circled the head lightly, spending extra time on the underside where he seemed to be most sensitive. She let him guide her, the pressure on her scalp stinging as he pushed further into her mouth. Her eyes watered as she adjusted to his size and panic clawed at her as he seemed to grow larger and larger.

"Relax your throat, baby. Breathe through your nose. That's it," he crooned in encouragement as she did what he asked. "Every time I hit the back of your throat I want you to swallow."

Bayleigh looked up at him beneath lowered lids, taking in the light sheen of sweat that coated his body and the way his muscles trembled. His cheeks were hollowed and his breathing harsh as he began to pull back. And it was then she realized just how much power she had—restrained or not.

She swirled her tongue again around his cockhead once he'd pulled almost all the way out and then she swallowed him down when he hit the back of her throat once more. His fingers tightened on her scalp and she moaned around him as she felt her own pleasure escalate. She tightened her lips around him as he thrust back inside her mouth, holding him prisoner as her tongue worked magic around his cock.

"Fuck, I'm going to come."

Bayleigh moaned and swallowed, her eyes watering as she felt him swell even more in her mouth. And when the sweet jets of come coated her throat all she could do was drink him down and wish for more.

He relaxed his grip on her head and pulled his still hard cock from her mouth slowly, his eyes dazed with pleasure, and she licked her lips, tasting him one last time.

***

Cade looked down at the siren in front of him and knew he was in trouble. He knew she didn't have a lot of great experiences with sex, or really all that much experience to begin with. At least, not on the same level he was used to. But she'd just swallowed him down like she'd been born to suck his dick, and damned if he wasn't looking forward to her doing it again.

But there was no way in hell he could go any longer without being inside of her. The last two weeks had been torture. He moved the pillows from beneath her head and moved them under her hips, enjoying the way the silk of her hair spread across his dark sheets. Her breasts were ripe and full before him, her arms still retrained, and that bare pussy was so wet he could see the cream coating her folds.

"Please, Cade," she begged. "I can't wait any longer."

He reached to the nightstand drawer and pulled out a condom, tossing it on the bed beside her before spreading her thighs wider. The pillows made it easier to see her fully—the pink folds of her pussy and her engorged clit peaking through the petals. His finger traced along the edges and her body arched, her head thrashing from side to side.

He couldn't resist the temptation, and his tongue

speared inside of her, tasting and lapping at the liquid passion that coated his tongue. She cried out and her hips jerked against him, the restraints around her wrists taut as her body bowed and shuddered. His finger pushed into her ass even as his tongue alternated between circling her clit and sliding inside of her. The sensation was too much, and her nectar filled his mouth. His cock grew even harder as she screamed her pleasure.

He rose up between her thighs, his cock jutting fiercely as he grabbed the condom and tore into the wrapping. He slid it on quickly and lifted her legs so her ankles rested on his shoulder.

"Christ, I can already feel the need to come again," he said, his voice so harsh he barely recognized it.

His eyes met hers as the thick head of his cock parted her folds. Her face was flushed and damp with desire and her breathing was irregular, panicked as she felt the size of him breach her tunnel.

"Relax, baby."

"I can't," she cried, her head shaking in denial even as he pushed inside her a little more. "It's too much."

"You'll take me, Bayleigh. Don't fight it." His thumb went to her clit and pressed down on the taut bud, and the ripples inside her pussy almost had him coming too soon. "Fuck, you're tight."

She relaxed around him bit by bit, and he didn't give her the chance to change her mind. He slammed inside of her to the hilt, her eyes widening at the invasion and then becoming dazed as passion overwhelmed her. He dropped her legs from his shoulders and arched over her, bracing his arms on either side of her body, his mouth going to her breast as he pummeled in and out of her.

This was heaven, he thought, scraping his teeth across her nipple and feeling her inner walls clench around him. Come boiled in his balls, but he held back, wanting to give her more pleasure. But when he looked into her eyes, it wasn't passion he saw there, but panic. She was thinking too hard. About what, he didn't know, but he'd noticed she was unsure of herself sexually. And he knew she believed she'd disappoint him, and that she was expecting not to be able to orgasm with him inside of her.

"Don't fight it, Bayleigh. Just feel. Feel my cock inside you. It's all that matters, baby. Nothing else."

He changed the angle of his thrusts so they were more shallow, hitting at a spot that had her jerking against him in surprise and wrapping her legs tight around his waist. Sweat dripped from his temples and he knew he wouldn't be able to last much longer.

"Now, Bayleigh. Now, goddammit."

The ripples around his cock started in slow undulations and then grew to pulsing waves as the orgasm exploded through her body. She screamed his name as he continued to drive into her tight flesh, and she tightened like a vise around him. There was nothing he could do to hold back his own release, and his back bowed and his skin tightened as he shot stream after stream of hot come inside of her. Never in his life had he regretted the use of a condom so fiercely. He wanted to own her. Possess her. And the thin latex had kept him from doing that.

He collapsed on top of her, barely having the forethought to catch his weight with his arm before he crushed her. Bayleigh lay limp beneath him, her eyes closed and her breathing ragged. She was out cold, and a smile twitched at his lips as he released her wrists from the restraints.

He went to the bathroom and discarded the condom, bringing back a warm cloth to wipe away the evidence of their lovemaking on her swollen skin. His phone buzzed from the pocket of his jeans and he picked it up, his expression grim as he read the text. He'd have two hours of downtime before he had to get back to work.

He looked at Bayleigh, still in the center of his bed, wondering what he was going to do with her. He hadn't made it a point of actually sleeping with his lovers over the last couple of years. Not since Carmen had a woman shared his bed. But even as he had the thought, Bayleigh rolled to her side and seemed to curl in on herself. She wasn't like the women he normally took to his bed. She was softer. Not as cynical. And she deserved to be held.

Cade sighed and blew the candle out on his nightstand before pulling Bayleigh into his arms and jerking the blankets over them. He could hold her for a little while. It's not like it was permanent. The reminder did little to ease his conscience as he snuggled against her, wondering if she was supposed to feel so right in his arms.

CHAPTER NINE

Cade slipped out of bed two hours later and dressed in the dark, leaving Bayleigh cocooned beneath the covers. He wore black cargo pants and a long-sleeved black t-shirt, and he pulled his hair back at the nape of his neck so it wouldn't get in his face.

The safe in his closet opened silently and he grabbed the two pistols he had on hand that weren't service weapons, and he stuffed extra ammo in his pockets and slipped night vision goggles over his head. He didn't believe in going into any situation unprepared, and he had no intention of dragging his captain or any of the local cops into his mess. It was his to clean up, and that's just what he was going to do.

He flipped off the lamp he'd left on in the living room and double checked all the windows and doors to makes sure there was no way anyone could see inside. He'd be back long before Bayleigh woke, but he still didn't want to take the chance that someone could pinpoint her so easily.

He snuck out of the house quietly, making sure his back yard was clear before heading down to the creek. He knew Declan was there, but the man was like a ghost, slipping in and out of the shadows like the mist over the water. A twig snapped to his left, and Cade knew Declan had made the noise deliberately to pinpoint his location.

His brother was dressed similarly in black, and Cade realized not for the first time how much they resembled each other in looks, much more so than Shane and Grant, who took after their mother. The only difference in his and Declan's coloring was their eyes. Dec's were an eerie shade of silver-gray that could turn cold as ice or hard as steel. He was also a couple of inches shorter than Cade, just topping an inch over six feet.

"There's a rise just on the opposite side of your street," Dec said by way of greeting. "It's heavily treed and there are plenty of good hiding places. They have a straight shot over your neighbor's house to yours. You keep all the lights off and the blinds closed so they're not seeing much except for your coming and going. On the other hand, your neighbor lady is another story. They can see straight through her house, and it wouldn't be hard for a good sniper to get a bead on her if that's what Carlos wanted. The only time they can't see in is when you go on your nightly visits."

Dec's brow raised in a silent question, waiting on Cade to tell him exactly what was going on during his nightly visits, but Cade chose to ignore him and ask his own.

"I thought you were leaving for an assignment." He followed Declan along the creek edge for about half a mile before his brother answered.

"It turns out you were the assignment." Dec turned back and Cade saw a flash of white teeth as his brother smiled. "My superiors had a feeling you'd try to draw Carlos out. They never believed for a second that you were serious about becoming a city cop. It's a good cover though. I've been keeping up with the cases you've handled the last couple of weeks. You've done a lot of good for them. Cleaned up a lot of messes. Captain Kelly is certainly impressed. Maybe you should stay on."

"I don't know," Cade said, shrugging. "It's different, that's for sure. I haven't been shot or stabbed yet. It's a nice change."

"Give it a few more days. I'm sure you'll have another scar to add to your collection."

They circled around and headed up the steep rise that looked down on his street. Carlos wouldn't put anyone too important on watch duty, not unless he was planning on escalating things by getting rid of Bayleigh. He had to take Declan's suggestion about a sniper trying to take her out to heart, but Carlos wasn't usually that impersonal. Carlos wanted Cade to suffer, and killing Bayleigh up close and personal would be the surest way to do that. If Carlos knew how much Bayleigh was beginning to mean to him then there would be no telling the extremes he would go to.

Cade watched Declan as he followed close behind him—the way he moved as if he were part of nature itself, his movements fluid, his intent deadly. More of a ghost than Cade could ever hope to be. And he wondered not for the first time exactly which part of the government Declan worked for. Dec had his fingers in a lot of pies, and he always seemed to be available to whatever organization needed him. He also didn't follow the same rules as regular agents were constricted to. Declan was a law unto himself.

They stopped at an outcropping of trees slightly above where Carlos' men had taken up position, and he and Dec used hand signals to indicate how many they saw. Cade's mouth tightened when he saw the sniper lying flat on the ground, completely focused, looking through the scope of his weapon in the direction of his house.

It was a damned good thing Bayleigh had been determined to avoid him and turn all her lights out, or she could have been dead before he'd gotten to her. Carlos was going to pay for this.

There were five men total, and Declan indicated with hand signals that he needed at least two of them alive to take back with him for questioning. Cade nodded reluctantly, but he understood the value of information. There were too many components of this mission left to destroy. They still had the scientists and labs to deal with. But the sniper wasn't going to be one of the survivors.

He and Declan moved as one, coming down on their targets from the top of the hillside and flanking them on either side. There was no need to use their guns, not when their hands were just as efficient a weapon.

Cade dispatched the sniper quickly, twisting his neck with deadly precision. He felt the air shift behind him, knowing another was coming up behind him, and he dodged just in time to avoid the wicked blade, so it sliced along his arm instead of into his back. But the sting in his flesh didn't stop him from achieving his goal. He finished the second man off quickly and then went to help Declan tie up and gag then two men he'd knocked unconscious.

"Go back to Bayleigh," Dec said. "My team will clean up this mess."

"Shit," Cade said, feeling the gash in his arm.

Blood soaked his shirt and dripped down his fingers. It was deeper than he'd thought, and there was no way he could get it patched up without Bayleigh finding out.

"You're going to have to make a decision where she's concerned, Cade. She doesn't even know what's going on here, or that you've thrown her life in danger. It seems like a hell of a chance to take for a woman that's just a meaningless fuck."

Cade had Declan by the front of his shirt and backed up against a tree before the red haze of anger could clear from his vision. He dropped his hand and ignored Dec's satisfied smirk. God, what kind of complete asshole was he? He'd decided as soon as he'd seen Bayleigh that he was going to have her.

There'd been too much desire between them to exert any kind of self-control. And he'd decided to take her, having every intention of it being a meaningless fuck or seven just as Declan had accused him of. Maybe if he hadn't just been inside her a couple of hours ago he'd still feel that way. But he had been inside her, and he'd known immediately that she wasn't going to be as easy to walk away from as he'd planned.

"You could walk away now and we could put her in a safe house. Carlos would forget about her as soon as you lost interest, and your attention wouldn't be splintered. I can already tell you're losing focus," Dec said, gesturing to the wound in Cade's arm. "She's innocent in this."

"I know that, dammit. But I'm not walking away yet. She knows the score, and came to the affair knowing I wasn't in it for a relationship. This isn't your business, Declan. I want one of your men on her when I can't be there. We keep her safe, Dec. It's non-negotiable. I'm not sending her away."

"It wouldn't kill you to admit that your feelings might run a little deeper than you want. You're allowed to be happy."

Cade scowled at his brother and turned his back on the words that cut into him like a knife. He walked down the way they'd come, back through the trees that surrounded his street in a private cocoon, and along the shallow creek bed until he reached his yard. Declan was right. He couldn't afford to have his focus splintered. He could keep Bayleigh safe and keep up their physical relationship as long as he didn't let emotion come into play.

***

Bayleigh knew Cade was gone the moment he'd gotten out of bed. She'd missed his warmth immediately, the touch of his hands across her stomach, holding her as if he'd been doing so forever.

She sure as hell could pick them.

It was going to hurt when their affair was over, no question about it. She'd already given too much of herself to him. He'd demanded too much. And now there was no way of taking it back. She wished she could approach an affair like a man—with no expectations or emotions involved—but she just wasn't built that way. And it was a mistake for her to try it with Cade.

She flipped on the bedside light and got out of bed, padding to his open closet doors to find a shirt since all she had with her was a damp bathing suit. Her body ached and throbbed in places she wasn't used to aching. Cade had taken her like none of her other lovers had before. He'd paid attention to her needs, worked to make sure she was satisfied.

She'd seen the tortured expression on his face as he held back, waiting for her to find fulfillment. It made her love him more. God, she was insane. She couldn't afford to love a man like Cade MacKenzie.

His shirt hung to her knees and she buttoned it slowly as she walked into the main living area of his house. It was dark as pitch inside, not a light on anywhere, and she wondered again what was going on. Cade wasn't in the house, and she'd glimpsed the weapon in his hand before he'd left the bedroom.

The back door opened silently, even as she had the thought, and Cade slipped back inside, his brow arching in surprise when he saw her standing there.

"Fancy seeing you here," she said. "I don't suppose you're going to tell me what this is all about, are you?"

He flicked the dead-bolt and headed into the kitchen, rummaging in the pantry for a bottle of whiskey, and Bayleigh hardly contained the eye roll. He blended in with the darkness, only his outline visible as he moved around with familiarity.

"You know, your people skills need work," she said. "You haven't been able to keep your mouth shut for the last week, barging into my house and trying to piss me off by disagreeing with me on every stance I have just to be contrary, and now all of a sudden you can't find anything to talk about. What are you hiding from me, Cade?"

Cade smiled at her, the flash of his white teeth disconcerting in the darkness, and he threw back the whiskey like it was water.

"Why do I need to talk when you do it enough for both of us?"

"If I was a normal woman, I'd probably be offended by that, but I have brothers. And I promise I've heard all the insults before. I also know when a man is being stupid and trying to stall the conversation. You might as well tell me what's going on. I can be persistent."

She heard his sigh and went to the wall to turn the light on, tired of being confined to the darkness.

"No, leave it off for now," Cade said.

"I'm not going to have this conversation with you in the dark."

"Then I'll light a candle."

He rummaged through another kitchen drawer until he came out with matches, and he lit the fat white candle that sat in the middle of his kitchen table.

"Are you okay?" she asked, the feeling that something was off tingling in the back of her mind.

"Never been better. Though I wouldn't mind a replay of earlier."

"Not until you start talking."

She watched Cade warily as he grabbed another glass from the cabinet and set it on the table, a challenging quirk fixed on his mouth. She took a seat and accepted the whiskey he pushed in front of her. And then he sat across from her, his features harsh in the candlelight, and she gasped. His face was slicked with sweat and there was pain in his eyes as he met her gaze. He knocked back the second glass and seemed to deflate against the chair.

"What happened, Cade? Are you hurt?"

She was up and around to his side in an instant, her fingers brushing the hair back that had fallen onto his brow. She held two fingers to the rapid pulse beating in his throat and then worked her way down until her fingers touched the sticky substance on his arm.

He hissed out a breath at her touch and poured more whiskey into the glass. "Don't touch it."

"You need a doctor."

"No, doctor. Not this time. We're safe here for the

night, but I don't want anyone to know I've been hurt. They'll take advantage of the weakness."

"Who will? What's going on, Cade?"

He sighed and rested his head against her chest, letting his guard down for the first time she'd seen. It made him almost human. As if he wasn't quite as hard as he wanted everyone to believe.

"I'm sorry, Bayleigh," he said, looking up at her, his eyes fathomless pools of black. "I'll be honest with you. You're in danger because of me. Because I couldn't keep my eyes and my hands off you."

"It wasn't just one sided, Cade. I couldn't keep my hands off you either. Now tell me what's going on."

"I was involved in an undercover operation a few years ago," he said softly. "I went into Miguel del Fuego's drug cartel with the purpose of taking them out of existence—from finding where the hidden compounds were, to the scientists, to the buyers in the US. I was one of the worst people in existence for three years because I had to prove that I was who I said I was. And believe me, I was very convincing."

Bayleigh could see the torture swirling in his eyes, the guilt over the things he'd had to do, and the sight broke her heart. No wonder he seemed so cold and distant. She'd be doing everything she could to close herself off from the past.

"It's okay, Cade. You don't have to tell me anything you're uncomfortable with," she said, regretting she'd practically forced him to tell her. "Let's go into the bathroom. I'll see what I can do for your arm."

She grabbed the bottle of whiskey and followed him into the small hall bath. It didn't go past her notice that he had them inside and the door closed before he flipped on the light. This bathroom was under the stairs, so there wasn't a window. He stripped off his shirt, and she winced as the gash came into view.

"I hate to say this, but you're going to have to see a doctor. You need stitches."

"Get it cleaned up and let me decide from there," he said stubbornly.

"Would it kill you to say please?"

He leaned against the vanity, his legs spread slightly apart, and he wrapped his arm around her, pulling her closer until she stood between his thighs. Her heart thudded in her chest, and just that quick she could feel herself dampening for him—with one touch.

"Please," he whispered against her lips, his tongue tracing the full bottom curve lightly before his mouth pressed against hers.

It was the first time he'd kissed her so gently, where the heat had a chance to begin as a small flame and grow into something more, rather than the immediate explosion she'd grown used to. She pushed away, hers eyes wide and her legs shaking.

"You didn't ask to use my shirt," he said. "It seems like your manners are as bad as mine."

"I'll make sure to give it back after I look at your arm." Her throat was dry as dust, and if he didn't stop circling his finger on the back of her thigh, just where his shirt ended, she was going to be a whimpering puddle at his feet. "Do you have a first aid kit?"

"Yeah," he said, blowing out a long breath, his arousal obvious behind the stretched fabric of his cargo pants. He pushed her back gently and bent down to grab the first aid kit from underneath the sink.

Bayleigh wet a washrag with warm water and cleaned away the blood. She'd seen her fair share of scrapes and cuts growing up with Brady and Brant, and she knew when a wound needed stitches. Stubborn man.

"Here," he said, shoving the whiskey she'd sat by the sink into her hand. "I don't have any antiseptic. This is as good as any."

Bayleigh took a quick swig from the bottle, grimacing as the liquor burned a path all the way down her throat and into her stomach.

"If you say so. Button up, buttercup."

She poured the amber liquid over the slice in his arm and winced right along with him as she imagined the burning pain he must be feeling.

"Sorry, sorry," she said, blowing on it like her mom used to do when they got cuts or scrapes. "I can see almost to the bone, Cade. You've got to get stitches."

"You sew, right?" he said, taking the bottle from her

hand and slugging it back. "Just pretend I'm a piece of sexy, delicate silk."

Bayleigh took a step back and stared at him in shock, the horror of what he was asking starting to penetrate. "Umm, I don't think—"

"We don't have a choice. I can't go to the hospital. The cartel that I was working undercover in has found me. The DEA didn't destroy it as fully as we'd hoped. Miguel's son has taken over the reins and he's here, and he's been in contact with me. He knows I'm interested in you, and you're in danger because of it. He'll stop at nothing to make sure that I pay for what happened. You need to understand the severity of the situation. This is life or death, Bayleigh."

"It seems a bit extreme to make me a target. We barely know each other."

Cade grasped her by the chin and made her meet his eyes. "He knows me well, Bayleigh. He knows I wouldn't normally pursue a woman like you unless—"

"Unless what?"

"I've got thread and a needle tucked into a pocket there," he said, changing the subject. "I need to get bandaged up and get a couple of hours sleep before the sun rises."

He grabbed the bottle of ibuprofen from the first aid kit and swallowed three of them, while Bayleigh took the needle and thread and swallowed the bile that threatened to rise in her throat. Her hands shook and little black dots starting flashing in front of her eyes.

"Take another drink and relax," he said. "Try not to think of it as flesh. Make your mind see it as something you're comfortable with."

"Easy for you to say."

"Not really. Did you notice the scar on my thigh?"

Bayleigh felt the heat rush to her cheeks and she busied herself by threading the needle. She'd noticed everything about his body. He laughed softly and she felt her face flame hotter.

"I didn't have anyone to sew that one together. That was a little reminder left by Miguel. His way of making sure I was as tough as he'd heard I was. I had to stitch myself together with my left hand. It didn't turn out pretty."

She took a deep breath and poured the whiskey over the needle before piercing his flesh. He didn't even wince as she began to make tiny stitches along the gaping wound.

"I thought you were left-handed," she said absently, focusing on the task at hand. "Why would that be a big deal?"

"No," he said, his voice strained even though he wasn't moving a muscle as she worked. "I got shot in the hand a few years ago, and I had damage to some of the tendons. I couldn't use it at all for a while, and I had to sit behind a desk until I could show I was proficient using my weapon with my left hand. It's part of the reason I was given the opportunity to go undercover in del Fuego's organization. I wasn't of any use as a field agent, and they needed someone unattached to infiltrate."

"I've got to tell you, I'm not a fan of the fact of how often you seem to get shot or stabbed. Maybe you need a new line of work."

"Yeah," he said, his sigh soft against her skin. "I've been thinking that a lot lately. But I can't do anything until the del Fuego cartel is in ashes."

"There," Bayleigh said, taking a step back, her stomach feeling queasy now that she was done.

Cade dug around in the First Aid Kit until he came up with some Neosporin, and he spread it liberally over her neat stitches. "Here, wrap me up. Not too tight," he said, handing her a roll of gauze.

Bayleigh wrapped the wound, and tried to process everything Cade had told her. She'd spent her entire life trying to escape the thought of the dangers her father and brothers faced on a daily basis. And here she was, thrown into a situation she had no control over and falling in love with a man who made her brothers seem like docile pets.

"I think I need to go home," she finally said after an awkward length of silence. "I've got to work tomorrow, and I haven't exactly had a restful night."

She handed him the supplies and turned to open the door, but his hand pushed against it before she could get it open. His body shifted, and she felt the presence of him looming over her back before his lips feathered across her ear. Shivers skittered over her skin before she could control her reaction.

"If you think I'm letting you go now," he whispered,

"After I've felt how you hold my cock like a glove, then you're in for a hell of a surprise."

CHAPTER TEN

"Cade, don't make this harder than it already is. I'm not built for this. You could make me fall in love with you."

He stiffened behind her, rejecting the words, even as they brought him satisfaction. He wanted her love. He just didn't know if he could return it. After Carmen, he wasn't sure he was capable of ever loving anyone again, and he hadn't even wanted to try because of the danger in his life. Not that his caution had helped him any this time. Bayleigh had drawn him in and he was facing a situation that could end up similar to when Carmen was killed. Only this time, he didn't think he'd be able to survive it. Bayleigh had wrapped herself around his heart that quickly.

Love wasn't something he could deal with just yet. He only knew he wanted Bayleigh to belong to him. And that it was his duty to keep her safe. Nothing else mattered right now.

His hand skimmed up the silky length of her inner

thigh, rubbing in slow circles, teasing at the sensitive flesh he knew was already wet and creamy for him. Her breath hitched as he nibbled at the spot just between her neck and shoulder, and he used his other hand to quickly undo the buttons of the shirt she'd borrowed from him.

She shuddered beneath his fingers and her head leaned against the bathroom door in defeat. She couldn't deny him, just as he'd never be able to deny her. He turned her around so she faced him and took her mouth quickly—the kiss hot and deep and wet. They were both panting for breath by the time they broke apart, and Cade took a step back before he lost control completely. He'd never lost control with a woman. Never let her take him to the point where rational thought disappeared and all that was left was the animal nature writhing inside of him, trying to break free and claim what was his.

The sight of her pressed back against the door almost had him coming in his pants. Her golden hair was tousled sexily around her face and her lips were swollen and red from his kisses. The dress shirt she wore gaped open, but it was caught just at the edge of her nipples on each side, tempting him with glimpses every time she inhaled. His gaze traveled down to the bare flesh between her thighs, dewy with desire.

He sank to his knees in front of her, his tongue seeking the sweet honey that coated her pussy, and he reveled in her cries as he sucked at her clitoris and speared inside of her with his tongue. Her hands tangled in his hair and her legs widened so she was able to thrust against his face. He pulled back some, alternating between gentle caresses and hard thrusts, keeping her just on the edge of fulfillment.

"Please, Cade. Stop teasing."

"But it's so much fun," he said, skimming his fingers along the delicate folds before sinking one long digit inside of her.

"Ahh," she screamed, clamping down on his finger, flooding his mouth with her desire as her orgasm drew nearer.

"You're so tight around my finger. I can't wait to feel you on my cock. You'll be swollen from the orgasm I'm about to give you, and I'll have to push my way inside you, inch by inch, as your pussy grips me like a fist."

"Please, please," she begged, almost sobbing with her need.

Cade withdrew his finger and then added a second as he pushed back inside of her, his mouth clamping on to the taut bud of her clit and sucking it, flicking it rapidly with his tongue, until he felt the explosion of her come against his taste buds. He drank her in until the spasms stopped and she collapsed against him in exhaustion.

He held her up with his good arm and leaned her against the vanity as he untied his boots and stripped out of the rest of his clothes. Her eyes were dazed and half-closed and he could see her heart pounding beneath those amazing breasts. His cock was hard and his balls were drawn up tight. Seeing her unravel in front of him hadn't done a lot for his control. He'd be lucky to last thirty seconds once he got inside of her.

"No more running from me, Bayleigh. No more denying what you feel. We're in this together, and I swear I'll keep you safe. You just have to trust me."

The shadows that clouded her eyes didn't go unnoticed, and he wished he could hunt down every one of the bastards that had convinced her she wasn't good enough—wasn't special in their arms. They'd whittled away at her self-confidence and undermined her sexuality to the point she had trouble even reaching an orgasm. He could still see her inner struggle the closer and closer she got to coming, and it broke his heart. As much as he demanded her trust, she still wasn't giving it to him. And he had to have her trust—no, her soul—to be able to do all the things he wanted to do to her, with her.

He slid open the glass door of the shower and turned on the water, making sure the temperature was nice and warm. Steam filled the room quickly and he went back to Bayleigh, taking her into his arms and kissing her softly, deeply, until she was pliant and needy against him once more.

"You shouldn't get your arm wet," she said as he led her into the shower, adjusting the nozzle so it didn't get her hair wet.

"It'll be fine, sugar. Just kiss me again. I'm so hard for you I ache."

She surprised him by nipping at his bottom lip, and he growled as pleasure shot straight to his cock. Her mouth was hot and aggressive as her tongue stroked along his own. Cade pumped soap into his hands and quickly washed the night's activities from his body, and he almost spilled into her hand when she grasped his cock in that tight little hand and started pumping.

"Enough, Bayleigh," he said, silencing her protest with his mouth.

He backed her against the cool tile wall of the shower and brought her leg up so it wrapped around his hip. The heat from her pussy enveloped his cock as he probed at the saturated folds. Her eyes fluttered closed as he pushed the swollen head inside of her, her inner muscles clamping around him and pulling him inside. She was so wet, so hot, so—unprotected.

"Fuck," he said, clenching his eyes closed in frustration. "Condom."

She tightened her leg around his waist and he slid inside a little further, the need to bury himself fully suddenly overwhelming.

"I'm on the pill. Don't stop. Please."

The inner struggle didn't last long. He knew birth control wasn't a hundred percent effective, but damned if he wanted to put latex between them now that he'd had a taste of what she felt like when they were flesh to flesh.

He groaned in surrender and plunged to the hilt inside of her, holding completely still once he got there because the come in his balls was boiling to the point of explosion and he wasn't ready for this to end yet. Her inner muscles quivered around him and he gritted his teeth, even as sweat dripped from his temples.

"Damn, you feel too good," he said, giving up on the battle.

He pulled out of her to the tip of his cock and then slammed back inside of her, swallowing her scream of pleasure with his mouth as he swelled inside her and shot thick streams of semen deep inside her. Part of him hated that she was on the pill—that need to mate and show his dominance by planting his seed inside of her all he could think of as he thrust inside her over and over again.

His lungs burned with the effort to breathe and he could tell that she was struggling to get control of herself. She hadn't orgasmed, but she was close.

"I'm sorry, baby," he said, pulling from her slowly, watching in awe as the combined fluids from their bodies dripped to the shower floor. "I'll fix it."

"What?" she asked, genuinely confused as he pumped more soap into his hand and gently cleaned between her thighs.

"You didn't get there. Just relax and I'll make sure we're even in no time."

"I don't have to get there, Cade. You give me more pleasure just being inside of me than I've ever had before. I don't expect to come every time. In fact, from what I've read, most women don't come every time they have sex. You don't have to take it as a personal challenge."

"Oh, but I do. If you don't come it means I haven't done my job right. And I'm always meticulous about getting the job done right."

He rinsed away the soap and turned her around so her breasts pressed against the tile. He trailed his fingers down her spine, enjoying the goosebumps that pebbled her flesh, and then further down between the cheeks of her ass, swirling once around the puckered star of her anus before dipping in to the drenched folds of her pussy.

He pulled her back some so her cheek and arms were braced against the wall and her ass was presented to him. His fingers teased and tormented as she writhed against him, seeking penetration.

"Christ, do you know how beautiful you look spread out like this? I'm getting hard again. Like a damned teenager. Only you do this to me, Bayleigh."

She shook her head in denial and whimpered as his fingers parted her folds and pushed inside. She took him in greedily and pushed back against his fingers, fucking them in a rhythm that had her moaning with pleasure.

He brought his other hand up and circled gently around her rear entrance, dipping down to her pussy and gathering juices, and then bringing them back up to lubricate the tiny hole. He sank his index finger inside slowly, stretching the unused portal until she was pushing against him, trying to take more.

"I'm going to take you here soon, Bayleigh."

He added a second finger, so he now had two in her pussy and two in her ass, and he worked them back and forth in tandem until her legs began to quiver from the strain of pleasure.

"I'll push inside your tight ass and sink all the way to my balls. You'll love it, baby. I can already tell. Your pussy is weeping right now, wanting what I can give you."

"Yes, yes," she hissed, her body jerking back and forth, searching for the satisfaction that seemed so elusive.

"Have you ever been fucked in the ass? Did your other lovers take you there?"

She shook her head, the words unable to be spoken.

"It's a shame," he said. "Maybe that's why you couldn't come for them."

He removed his fingers from her pussy and replaced them with his cock. It was as hard as it had been the first time he'd taken her. He pushed inside of her slowly, his only purpose this time in giving her the release she craved. His hand slipped beneath her, plucking at her turgid nipple as his thrusts grew deeper, harder.

"Cade," she chanted over and over again.

He kept his thrusts steady even as his fingers kept working in and out of her ass, and he brought his other hand down until it cupped her weeping pussy. His fingers plucked at her clit, strumming and circling the engorged nub until he felt the ripples of her inner walls around his cock.

"Yeah, baby," he whispered. "Come all over me. Drench me in that sweet pussy juice."

His naughty words sent her over the edge and her screams were silent as passion swept through her. Her cunt clenched around him and her ass tightened on his fingers. Wave after wave ripped through her until he could no longer hold his own orgasm back. He gripped her by the hips and fucked her hard before his come coated her insides.

He caught his hand on the wall above her head and hunched over her, hoping to God he wouldn't embarrass himself by collapsing to the floor. The sight of her face had a smile quirking at his lips. He was pretty sure she was asleep on her feet. He pulled out of her with a groan and cleaned them both up, all the while holding her lax body against him.

"Come on, baby. Time for bed."

She burrowed against him, her cheek fitting just under his chin, and he felt the lock snick open on his heart.

"Shit," he whispered, closing his eyes and looking up at the ceiling. He wasn't ready. As long as he kept that little bit of distance between them, she'd never know how much control she had over him. Because at that moment, he was willing to give her everything.

CHAPTER ELEVEN

"I have to go to work, Cade. You can't just keep me locked up in the house because you've decided I'm in danger."

Bayleigh poured a cup of coffee and dug around in his pantry for something edible. She came out with a half a loaf of bread and an empty box of cereal. She checked the fridge and saw he had a few bottles of beer and two eggs and she sighed in disgust. Her brothers' refrigerators always looked the same.

"I thought I explained this already. Bad men are out to get us. They have a dangerous drug that has already killed three women in the area. Carlos told me he was coming after you," he said, ticking off each item on his fingers as his anger seemed to grow. "And you think it's a good idea to go traipsing off to work like you don't have a care in the world? Have you lost your mind?"

Cade sat at the table with his own coffee, his hair still

damp from his shower, and only wearing a pair of worn jeans that were driving her crazy. The last thing she was ready to do was talk about what they'd done during the night, but he wasn't likely to let her forget. And he wasn't letting her put distance between them, constantly pulling her into his arms for kisses that shook her to the core.

She grabbed the eggs and the bread and dug around the kitchen until she found a frying pan. She cracked and beat the eggs and then soaked the bread it in before making French toast. She didn't answer him until she brought the food to the table and sat across from him.

"I own a business. I have responsibilities. And I have client appointments today. I can't just throw away thousands of dollars in income because you think I might be in danger."

He narrowed his eyes at her. "I don't *think* you're in danger. You *are* in danger. And I don't see why you have to be so stubborn about this. Maybe your brothers can convince you to use your common sense."

Bayleigh got up from the table and walked slowly toward Cade, the shirt she'd stolen from him barely buttoned and enticing him with every step. His pupils dilated with desire and she watched his cock swell beneath his jeans. She moved as if she were going to straddle his lap, but at the last second moved her knee so it was pressed directly against his balls. His indrawn breath was enough to know that she was using the right amount of pressure.

"Don't you ever threaten me with my brothers," she whispered in his ear. "I get enough of that from them, and I won't take it from you too, no matter how much control you think our sleeping together gives you. I'm old enough to make my own decisions and take the consequences of my actions. I control my life. No one else."

She nipped at his ear and felt satisfaction at his indrawn breath. After the night they'd spent together she'd discovered very quickly that Cade wouldn't break down her confidence as her previous lovers had. If anything he'd empowered her to start taking control of the men in her life. Boy were they all going to be in for a surprise.

She kissed him once and then moved back to her side of the table, taking a bite of her breakfast, and ignoring the predatory look in his eyes. She'd pay for her little stunt later, and damned if she wasn't looking forward to it.

"I need to get back home and change clothes. As much as I like wearing your shirt, I think my clients would be a bit scandalized."

"They'd be jealous. I'd rather see you wearing that shirt than the fancy lingerie you sell. It's sexy as hell. Especially since I know you're not wearing underwear."

"Oh, really?" she asked. "And I was looking forward to showing you some of the new items I just got in."

"You're playing with fire, Bayleigh. I promise you don't want to keep pushing me."

"Your threats don't scare me, Cade. Now walk me home so I can get ready for work."

"Only if you let me drive you and pick you up," he said.

"I want you to be safe."

"Fine. I've been looking for some part-time help. You'd probably be good at selling ladies' underwear. You seem to know an awful lot about it."

Humor filled her as she saw the uncomfortable look in his eyes. Teasing Cade was more fun than she'd thought it would be. It was nice to be the one keeping him off balance for a change.

"You realize I'm going to show no mercy the next time I get you naked, don't you?"

"That's what I was hoping," she said, laughing as he led her back to her house.

***

Ten hours later, the last thing Bayleigh wanted to do was laugh. She'd shown up to her shop to find that Cade had instituted a bodyguard inside her store who made her clients more wary than curious, and several of them had left before even getting the chance to browse. And if that wasn't bad enough, two of her scheduled fittings hadn't shown, and neither of them had bothered to call to let her know they weren't coming.

By the time Cade came in to pick her up that evening, her temper had reached the boiling point.

"You ready to go?" he asked, ignoring her response to get a report from the guard dog he'd sicced on her.

Bayleigh locked the front door and grabbed her purse

and sewing bag—since she had several projects she was going to have to spend more time working on at home—and she went to wait by the back door for Cade, her foot tapping impatiently.

Damned, high-handed man, she thought.

She'd gone from living a perfectly normal life to jumping at shadows and watching everyone that passed by her doors with suspicion just because she'd had the bad luck of having Cade MacKenzie move next door to her.

He came toward her, still talking quietly to the watchdog, his eyes watchful as he took in her mood. His steps slowed the closer he got. It was obvious by the look on his face he remembered perfectly well where her knee had ended up that morning, and he wasn't looking to repeat the experience.

"What's wrong, Bayleigh?"

"Other than the fact that you have me under lock and key, and I can barely go to the bathroom without Neanderthal man standing outside the door and listening to me pee? I didn't agree to this, Cade. He's scaring off my customers."

She could tell by the twitch of his mouth that he wanted to laugh, and she swore that if she heard even one chuckle she was going to belt him right in the nose. She turned her narrow-eyed gaze to the Neanderthal in question just to make sure he didn't make the mistake of following Cade's lead. He paled appropriately under her stare and she nodded her head in satisfaction.

"Take me home, Cade, and then kindly take your cartels and stupid agency high-handedness and jump off the nearest cliff. I don't care how good the sex is. I can't live like this."

Neanderthal man choked on his laughter and brought his hand up to rub across his mouth to cover his smile. Cade wasn't nearly so amused.

"Now listen here, sweetheart," he said, taking a step toward her, but she put her hand to his chest and pushed him back as she heard her cell phone ringing from the bottom of her purse. She sighed as she saw who was on the other line. One of her no-show clients of the day.

"Ginny," she said, answering the phone with false sweetness. "I'm so glad to hear from you. I was starting to worry."

Bayleigh listened to the other woman's half-assed excuses about how her society schedule was just so packed with luncheons and charity events that she'd forgotten all about Bayleigh's cute little shop. Bayleigh gritted her teeth in annoyance, trying to remember that Ginny Van Sice had ordered enough lingerie for her third wedding/honeymoon that Bayleigh would be able to pay two full months of expenses from the purchase. All she had to do was let Ginny feel superior and listen to her bragging. It was a small price to pay for the result.

By the time she hung up the phone and had rescheduled Ginny for later in the week, a headache was brewing behind her eyes, and all she wanted to do was go home, open a bottle of wine and sleep for twelve hours. Cade sure as hell hadn't let her get a lot of sleep the night before.

"What was that all about?" Cade asked.

"I had two clients scheduled for fittings today that decided not to show," she said, following Cade out to his truck, trying not to be intimidated by the way the two men flanked both sides of her to keep her safe. "It's a common occurrence with Ginny. It's Becca I'm worried about. She'd never missed an appointment, and she's not the flighty type like Ginny is. She's a sweet girl."

Cade got into the truck cab and started the engine, pulling out first and letting the guard trail behind them.

"What's her full name and address?" he asked, pulling out her phone and hitting speed dial.

"Becca Whitson. Short for Rebecca," she said, pulling up Becca's personal information on her iPad.

Bayleigh read off the address to Cade and watched him curiously.

"Yeah, this is MacKenzie," he said into the phone. "Can you do a drive by and check out an address for me?" Cade rattled off the address and hung up the phone. "Are you hungry? I haven't had a chance to eat dinner yet."

"Yeah, that's fine. Why are you having someone check on Becca?" Bayleigh asked, fear starting to creep across her skin and cling to her body like the sticky weaving of a spider web.

"You said she was a reliable client. My gut just had a

twinge, and I've learned over the years not to ignore it. I'm sure she's fine. How about Chinese?" he asked, driving through a strip mall where there were several different restaurants.

"Sure."

They got a table and ordered, but the silence was strained between them. She chewed at her bottom lip, wondering if she'd somehow gotten Becca in trouble. Her nerves were working overtime and her appetite was non-existent. She'd done nothing but push the food around on her plate since it had arrived.

"Bayleigh, look at me," Cade said softly.

She forced herself to meet his gaze, felt the emotion settle over her as she saw the sympathy and compassion in his gaze.

"None of this is your fault, sweetheart. You're just an innocent bystander. If this is anyone's fault it's mine for not staying away from you when I knew I should have. But I took one look at you and knew I wasn't that strong. You can't control what other people do, especially when those other people are pure evil. Just stay with me, and I'll keep you safe."

"For how long, Cade?" she asked sadly, knowing the answer before he even spoke the words.

"For as long as I can, love. For as long as I can."

The drive back to her house was made in silence, and Cade kept checking his phone, almost willing it to ring. But there was no word from whomever he'd contacted to check on Becca. Cade parked his truck in his garage and then he led her through his house, turning on a few lights as they went, before leading her out the back door and over to her own house.

"Carlos has men watching the house," he whispered as he unlocked her back door. "But my brother and some of his men are keeping them contained for the moment, tracking their movements. They still haven't caught sight of Carlos. He's who we're after, and he's a slippery bastard for a lunatic."

She'd left several lights on throughout the house, and all her blinds were still down from when Cade had lowered them earlier that morning. She went directly to the fridge and pulled out a bottle of white wine, pulling out the cork with expert movements and pouring herself a full glass. Cade grabbed a beer and stared at her warily, obviously unsure how to handle her in this particular mood.

"So are you staying here tonight?" she asked once the wine was gone and her body began to relax.

Cade looked at her in surprise. "I figured you were going to try and come up with some lame excuse for us not to sleep together again."

"I was," she said shrugging. "But like you said, the sex is good. Why not enjoy while it lasts?"

CHAPTER TWELVE

Cade made sure his face didn't betray his feelings, keeping it carefully blank as Bayleigh made her announcement with all the enthusiasm of reciting a grocery list. When she referred to what they had between them as just good sex, it left a bitter taste in his mouth and an anger that wanted to refute her words. But that's what he'd wanted. Just mindless sex for as long as it lasted, no emotions, and she was giving it to him in spades.

She unbuckled the wide black belt that cinched her waist, letting it drop to the floor, and then pulled the red cashmere tunic over her head as she went past him and headed toward the bedroom. She tossed the sweater onto the couch as she passed by and his lungs tightened in his chest as he saw what she was wearing beneath.

He followed behind her slowly, the sway of her hips erotically hypnotic, and his cock was swollen to the point that just the touch of his boxers was painful against the sensitive skin. She unzipped the long black skirt she wore and it slithered down her legs, leaving her in the tall, black leather stiletto boots and the most incredible underwear he'd ever seen in his life.

"Sweet Jesus," he whispered reverently as she turned around to face him.

"You like it?" she asked, her voice throaty as she purred the question. "I just got it in this morning."

Answering was out of the question. He was having a hell of a hard time catching his breath, and even his skin felt like it was too tight for his body. The corset she wore was fuck me red, and it plumped her breasts to impossible heights, making his cock jump at the thought of what it would feel like to thrust between the abundant mounds of flesh. Her waist was small and one hand was cocked on her flared hip in a pose meant to showcase every line and curve of her body.

She wore a matching red lace thong and he could see her desire dampening the fabric from where he was standing. Garters came down and fastened to the black thigh-highs she wore, and the tall boots came to just above her knees and fit her like a second skin. If she'd been holding a whip he might have fallen to his knees in submission. As it was, he could see the flickers of doubt in her eyes as she let him look his fill, and he knew this was going to be an important moment in their relationship—a shifting of power—a mutual satisfaction and need that neither of them might be prepared for.

"You take my breath away," he said, peeling off his

shirt and enjoying her reaction to his body as her eyes filled with lust. He kicked off his shoes and unbuckled his belt, pulling it from the loops slowly, her eyes mesmerized by his every movement. He unbuttoned his jeans, giving some much needed room for his cock, but he didn't remove his pants. Not yet. This would be over much too soon if he didn't try to keep some kind of control over the situation.

"How many of those contraptions do you have?" he asked, pointing to the corset and panties she wore.

"A whole store full," she said, arching a brow. "I didn't realize you wanted to talk tonight. I can just put on my robe if you'd like."

Cade smiled at the challenge in her voice and walked closer. "It doesn't matter what you wear, sweetheart. It's all going to end up on the floor anyway."

He moved quickly, catching her gasp against his mouth as he pushed her against the wall and tore the lace thong from her body. His fingers plunged into her just as his tongue plundered her mouth and she drenched his hand immediately, screaming out her orgasm as she shuddered and spasmed against him.

"That's it, baby," he said, kissing his way down her neck to the sensitive mounds of her breasts, his tongue laving just at the edge of where flesh met satin. He pushed his jeans down so they fell around his ankles and stepped out of them, and he tightened his grip around her hair as he pushed her lower.

"You know what I want, Bayleigh."

His voice was rough and graveled and her eyes were wide and open on his as she slowly knelt down in front of him, her nails raking across his thighs and drawing his balls into tight knots of anticipation.

He kept his gaze steady on hers as she licked her lips once before taking his cock in her hand and pumping it slowly, and he watched as the blue of her eyes darkened as she licked the tiny drop of pre-cum that had beaded at the head. He felt that one lick zing through his balls all the way down to his toes, and he groaned as she kissed and nibbled her way down to the hairless sac below, rolling them gently in her mouth and then kissing her way back to his cockhead again.

There was no warning when she opened her mouth and swallowed him whole, relaxing her throat and taking him all the way down until her chin touched his scrotum. He held her there, pressing against her scalp, as she swallowed against him repeatedly, her tongue laving the underside of his cock.

"Fuck, I could come already," he said, dropping his head forward and leaning one arm against the wall for support.

She moaned around him, the vibrations like an electric shock up his shaft, and she sucked him harder, bringing her other hand up to caress his balls. The duel sensations brought him closer to orgasm. He could feel the tightening at the base of his spine, the impending pleasure that crackled across his skin and shot tingles from his scalp to his toes.

"I'm going to come, Bayleigh. Take all of me, baby," he commanded, holding her head tight as he began to fuck her mouth with short, hard strokes.

The groan that erupted from his chest surprised him in its intensity and his vision went dark as he spurted stream after stream of thick semen down her throat.

His knees threatened to give out as pleasure like he'd ever known rocketed through his body, and he pulled his still hard cock from the soft suction of her mouth. She licked the last drop of his essence from her lips and smiled seductively, her eyes glazed with passion.

"I need you, Cade. Don't make me wait."

"I'll give you what you need, sweetheart. Stand up," he said, helping her keep her balance as she rose to her feet, and he led her over to the bed, still dressed in everything but the underwear he'd torn from her body.

"Lay down," he ordered, the rough edge in his voice wracking her body in shivers of anticipation.

"What are you going to do to me?"

"Patience, sweetheart."

He unzipped one of her boots and pulled it from her foot slowly, sinuously, rubbing at the arch of her foot until she was purring in pleasure. He did the same to the other foot and took her boots to the closet, where he riffled through the selection of scarves she had folded neatly on a shelf.

He picked one of the longer ones, the fabric so soft it felt like a second skin, and his cock jumped as he watched her eyes fill with anticipation and the tiniest bit of trepidation. She bit her lip and shifted on the bed.

"Cade," she said, shaking her head as he folded the scarf length-wise and covered her eyes, tying it securely at the back of her head. "I don't know—"

"Ssh, sweetheart. It's just me. All you have to do is feel."

He stood back and just took in the sight of her. Red satin and pale skin—like every man's wet dream. She was so beautiful. Outspoken and sarcastic and so fucking sexy he could barely draw in a breath when she was near. She wasn't afraid to go head to head with him if she disagreed about something. And that one sliver of vulnerability that came into her eyes whenever she thought she was disappointing him in some way drove him crazy. It made him want to hunt down her ex-fiance and do bodily harm, because the man had obviously had no idea what a treasure he had. She was Cade's perfect match in every way—intellectually and sexually—and it scared the hell out of him.

"Do you know how beautiful you are, Bayleigh?" he asked, skimming his fingers over the smooth skin of her neck and down to toy with the top of the corset that tempted him beyond reason.

He pushed the satin cups down so her breasts popped free—plump and swollen and ready for his mouth—and his fingers traced around the taut nipples that were drawing tighter and tighter with desire.

The bare folds of her pussy glistened with desire and he

couldn't help but lean down and kiss the creamy lips, tonguing the sensitive bud gently over and over again. He held her hips still as she began to writhe against him, searching for more, and he dipped his tongue lower, slipping into the quivering depths of her pussy as her sweet cream exploded against his tongue.

"Oh, God. Please," she begged. "I'm so close."

"I know," he said, the satisfaction evident in his voice. He blew cool air across her heated skin and watched her flesh pebble. "The good things in life are worth waiting for, baby."

He moved up her body to the trembling mounds of her breasts, laving his tongue across the turgid peak of her nipple and sucking it deep. Her hands went to his head, pulling him closer, but he gathered her wrists with one hand and held her down, wanting to give her everything he could before he lost control.

His other hand moved back down to the drenched folds of her pussy, and he slid two fingers inside of her, reveling in the sound of his name falling from her lips as she adjusted to his invasion.

"Come for me, baby," he whispered, biting down on her nipple with enough pressure that he felt her tighten around him.

She liked that edge of pain. Almost needed it to get off. He curved his fingers up slightly so they pressed against the most sensitive spot inside of her and she dissolved like liquid pleasure all around him.

"Cade," she moaned, fighting against the hold he had on her hands as she thrust against his fingers. She came apart in his arms, her whole body one sensitized nerve ending, as she soaked his fingers with her release. A light sheen of sweat coated her body as she came down from the tremors of her orgasm, and her breath hitched as he pulled out of her.

"Please, Cade. I need you."

Her voice shook as if she were on the brink of tears, and he had to fight the need to pull her close and not push her any further. He needed her to understand this side of him, but he couldn't afford to lose himself inside her. It was a shaky tightrope he was walking. Demanding all and not giving too much.

"You'll get me, sweetheart."

He cleared all of the pillows from her bed and lifted her gently, pulling back the white down comforter so it fell to the floor. The drawer of her nightstand held exactly what he'd been looking for, and her hands automatically went to the blindfold when she heard him rummaging around inside.

"Don't touch it," he commanded. "This all stops the minute you remove that blindfold."

"That's not fair, Cade. I want to see you. I want to touch you too."

"Not tonight, baby. Every inch of you is mine. Any and every way I want you."

She hesitated before nodding once and lied back down

in the center of the bed. Cade unhooked the garters from her hose and pulled the silk thigh-highs from her legs, using the stockings to bind her wrists to the curved iron of her headboard. There was still plenty of give in the stockings so he'd be able to move her around as needed.

"I'm going to turn you over," he whispered, kissing her hip before rolling her to her stomach.

His own control was slipping, to the point that his body shook with the effort to hold back the severity of his need. His cock had never been so hard, and it stood out from his body, thickly veined and throbbing for another release. He made quick work of the row of tiny hooks down her spine, and the corset fell away, leaving her in nothing but the red lace garter belt, framing her ass and making his mouth water.

He lifted her and tossed the corset to the floor before moving between her legs, kissing and licking his way down her spine, his fingers plucking at her nipples as she tried to move against him.

Sweat coated his skin and his muscles trembled with need. The game was over. He couldn't wait any longer. Not if he wanted to survive. He grabbed two of the pillows he'd thrown to the floor and put them beneath her stomach, so her ass was put on display.

"God, baby. You're so wet for me."

His fingers dipped inside of her, gathering her moisture before bringing it up to the virgin hole of her rear entrance. She whimpered as his finger slid easily inside, and she pushed against him as he began to stretch her, adding another finger to the first.

He couldn't resist her weeping pussy, and he laid on his back, keeping his fingers in her ass, as he tongued the moist folds, sucking and nibbling, his fingers working in and out of her back entrance as she rode his face with abandon. He could tell she was just on the edge of orgasm and he pulled his fingers free and moved from beneath her.

"Cade," she yelled. "Please don't stop. Don't—"

Her sobs of need pushed him to the breaking point, and he grabbed the vibrator she kept in her drawer and the tube of lubricant he'd also found. He spread her thighs and pushed the thick device into the weeping depths of her pussy all the way to the hilt. She gasped, her breaths ceasing, at the invasion, but she took it in easily.

"Fuck, that's sexy," Cade said, turning on the device to the lowest setting, just enough to push her closer to the edge. Not drive her over.

He squeezed the tube of lubricant directly into her back hole, massaging and working it inside until she was pushing against him, eager for his touch.

"Take a deep breath and relax, baby. Open yourself and push against me."

Sweat popped out on his brow and his teeth clenched in restraint as he pushed the swollen head of his cock past the tight ring of muscle inside her anus. Her hands clawed at the mattress, and mewls of pleasure escaped from her lips even as she cried out from the sharp edge of pain.

He worked himself inside her slowly, giving her time to adjust before pulling out and pushing back in again. Come boiled in his balls and his muscles quivered as he lost that last edge of sanity, the last bit of control he had, and plunged inside her to the hilt, his balls slapping against her ass. He didn't take time to gasp for breath but just started moving without restraint, his control shot to hell.

Her screams of pleasure spurred him on as he felt for the button on the vibrator that would kick it up a notch. He could feel the vibrations tickling his cock against the thin wall between her pussy and rectum, and he knew there was no way he could hold back any longer. He grabbed her hips and slammed inside her over and over again, his head thrown back and his body a machine.

"Fuck," he yelled as he felt her tighten around his cock, her orgasm strangling him until he thought his cock would be bruised from the pressure.

"Cade—Cade," she screamed. "I love you—"

Her words had his body stiffening, but it was already too late. It was as if he'd been waiting for her declaration, and his orgasm didn't start in any one place and roll through his body like the orgasms he'd had before. He shouted as his release exploded through him with a flash of light and pain and yearning, and he filled her ass with stream after stream of come, until he was just a husk of what he had been.

He collapsed on top of her, noticing she was out completely, her body so overwhelmed from the pleasure that she'd had no choice but to escape in a faint. He pulled out of her slowly and turned off the vibrator before pulling it from her and placing it on the nightstand. He barely had the energy to get up and shower quickly before coming back out and grabbing the comforter he'd thrown to the floor. Exhaustion crept over him as he pulled her into his arms and curled around her in sleep.

Sleep was just about to claim him when she rolled over in his arms, her eyes wide and shadowed, her skin cool to the touch.

"I meant what I said, Cade. I love you."

Pain reached up and vised around his heart until it was difficult to breathe. "I know you think you do," he said. "But I told you this is all there could ever be between us. Love isn't worth it, sweetheart. No matter how much you think you need or want it. Real love is painful. And it doesn't last forever."

He closed his eyes so he wouldn't have to look at the myriad of emotions that crossed her face—compassion, disappointment, pity. She made him feel as if he was the one in the wrong.

"Tell me about her," she whispered, stroking his face softly. "The one you lost."

CHAPTER THIRTEEN

Bayleigh's heart felt as if it were shattering into a million pieces. She knew going in that he would be the one man who'd make her risk everything—give everything. And with the way he'd just commanded her body and filled her to the point of breaking, he'd accomplished her greatest fear. She belonged to him mind, body and soul. But he didn't want her. Not really. Not when it counted.

His body had stiffened against hers at the mention of his dead lover, and he closed his eyes against the pain. She ached for him even as she wanted to push him away, but she couldn't put her love for him away just because he didn't return it. She loved him with everything she was, and what she felt for him didn't hold a candle to what she'd felt for Paul.

She knew Cade cared for her. He'd taken the time to get to know her quirks and her temper. He'd engaged her mind, and had spent time with her outside of the bedroom.

And the way he looked at her when he was buried deep inside of her, as if she were the only woman in existence. That seed of affection was there. Maybe he was too scared to love. She couldn't give up on him yet. Not if she really loved him.

"You loved her?" she asked, brushing the hair back from his face gently.

"Yeah," he said, meeting her gaze directly, the stark pain of memories showing in the harsh lines of his face. "I loved her."

She soothed him as best she could, her hands stroking his cooling flesh, wishing she could bear part of his burden.

"Carmen was—" he cleared his throat once and swallowed back the emotion. "She was the one bright spot in my life during the three years of hell I spent under Miguel's command. I knew about her before going undercover, and I'd planned from the beginning to seduce her and use her for information." Cade laughed bitterly. "But those thoughts didn't last long once I got to know her. She hated her father. Hated what he was doing, and she wanted to see him taken down. It took me three days to fall head over heels in love with her. It was one of those moments in time that just freezes in the brain—as if when I saw her everything went in slow motion and I just knew. I'd never been in love before, but I knew that she was it for me."

Bayleigh's heart clenched at his idea that he could only love like that once, but she stayed silent.

"I told you before the kind of person I had to be to

survive in the cartel. There's so much blood on my hands, Bayleigh," he said, bringing them up in front of his face, turning them over as if he could actually see the blood there. "I'd come back from job after job, each one just another fucking test that Miguel would make me do, and Carmen would be there. She'd know what I'd just done, and she'd take me into her arms anyway. Help me forget."

"I'm glad she was there for you," Bayleigh said softly. "I'm glad you had the comfort she gave."

Cade's hand tightened on her back and she cuddled closer.

"What happened to her?"

His sigh was so full of sorrow she almost wished she could take the question back. Almost. She needed to hear it all. And he needed to say it.

"I still don't know what happened completely. Someone betrayed me, and my brother, Declan, has been looking into it quietly, but whoever the mole was, he's buried deep and Dec hasn't found him yet."

"Whoever betrayed me told Miguel I was working undercover, and he also found out Carmen was feeding me information to turn over to the DEA. Miguel had us dragged out of bed in the middle of the night. They beat us both, and I was shot when I tried to protect her." His voice was cold and emotionless now, as if the memory were too much for him to bear. "One of Miguel's soldiers raped Carmen as they held me down. There was nothing I could do but watch."

His voice went hoarse and Bayleigh felt the tears as they

ran down her cheeks. "I'm so sorry, Cade."

She didn't want to hear anymore, but he didn't seem to be able to stop now that he'd started talking.

"Those same soldiers dragged us to the warehouse we used to hold shipments before they went out to the distributers. I knew we were going to die then. I'd been a part of the cartel too long. The warehouse was where we took anyone who needed to be disposed of. There were drains in the floor, so it was easy to clean up the messes," he said hollowly. "Carmen didn't know that, but I did. They'd kill us both and I was powerless to stop them. In the end it was Miguel who pulled the trigger. He looked me right in the eyes as he killed his only daughter—not an ounce of remorse in his eyes."

Bayleigh swallowed painfully, her heart breaking for him. "How did you get out?"

"My brother," he said, the hint of a smile softening his face. "Declan knew something was wrong when the shipment drop schedule was changed. He and I have been working together a long time. Your brother was there too."

"Which brother?" She thought quickly and realized that was probably a stupid question. There would be no reason for a Navy SEAL to be working a job stateside. And then she thought about what he'd just admitted. "You know Brant?"

"Mmm," he acknowledged, playing with the ends of her hair. "We went to college together."

"You do realize that at some point in the future when I

have the energy, I'm going to be irritated by this information?"

"I'd expect nothing less."

Bayleigh leaned up and took his face between her hands, seeing the surprise that came into his eyes as she kissed him softly on the lips. She felt the prick of tears once more as she saw the way he blanked his face, as if he couldn't deal with any more emotion.

"I'm so sorry for what he did to her," she said. "And I'm glad that you had the chance to experience the love that so many people never do. I know exactly the feeling you described. That moment where your life changes in an instant. Because it's how I felt when I met you. I love you, Cade."

His eyes filled with pain and sorrow and regret, and he shook his head, she was sure getting ready to deny that those were her true feelings.

"You don't have to say it back." She put her fingers across his lips to keep him from speaking. "All you need to know is that it's there if you want it. When you need it. I've had a relationship where there was nothing but accusations and hard words, where there was no respect. I know the difference now, and I know I can never settle for anything less. Paul didn't make me less because I wasn't what he needed. But you have made me more, Cade. And I'll always love you for that alone."

"I wish—" he said, moving her hand and pulling her closer so she leaned over him, her hair curtaining their faces.

"I wish I could give you more. But I just can't go through that again. Love hurts, Bayleigh. That's what the Hallmark Channel doesn't tell anyone. It hurts like nothing else in this world. I can care for you. I *do* care for you. But I just don't think I can let myself take the chance again."

She knew he wouldn't be pushed. This was something he was going to have to figure out on his own. All she could do was love him in every way she knew how. She crawled over him so her legs straddled his hips, and she leaned down to kiss him again.

"It's okay, Cade," she whispered. "You don't have to explain. Just let me love you."

He was already hot and hard beneath her, his cock nudging at her swollen folds as she kissed him deeper, her mouth sucking and stroking his tongue with slow, sensual motions. She rocked against him slowly, teasing herself every time his cock pressed against the taut bud of her clit.

"God, Bayleigh," he groaned, his voice tortured.

"Just let me love you," she said again before she sank down on him to the hilt in one smooth motion.

They moaned in tandem and she placed her knees securely on either side of him as she sat back so the penetration was deeper. He nudged at her cervix and she pressed down harder to feel the sensation again, squeezing and relaxing her muscles around him, but not letting him move inside of her as he wanted to do.

"You're killing me, baby."

His eyes were only half open, so black she could almost see herself in their depths, and his breathing was labored. His fingers bit into her hips, but she didn't mind the pain. This was a gift she could give him. Her love. Her need.

Her hands trailed over his chest, the ridged muscles jumping beneath her touch, and then they continued on, up her thighs and belly to her aching breasts. He watched her every movement, and sweat popped out on his brow as she took her nipples between her fingers and plucked them to hard points.

"Mmm, Cade," she moaned. "I could come just like this."

"If you don't move soon I'm going to spank that pretty ass until burns."

"You promise?" Her smile was wicked, but she decided to put him out of his misery. Her own orgasm was too close to play any longer.

His hand moved between her thighs, rubbing her clit in slow circles, and her head dropped back on her shoulders as sensations rioted through her body. Then she began to move. Her hips lifting, until the head of his cock was barely inside of her, and then falling again. She kept up the steady strokes, using her inner muscles to milk him as she rose up and down. Up and down. His fingers flicked faster, and she tweaked her nipples until she could feel the spasms start in her womb.

"I'm going to come, love. I can't hold back."

His hands went back to her hips and he began to thrust

up in to her with hard, fast strokes, until she was coming undone around him, crying out his name with her release even as he cried out hers. She felt his seed jet against her inner walls and her orgasm rolled into another and another.

She collapsed to his chest, their breathing heavy and erratic, and he pulled the covers over them and put his arms around her. Bayleigh was asleep before she could see the pain in Cade's eyes.

"If I could love anyone it would be you," he whispered.

CHAPTER FOURTEEN

The air shifted subtly, and the silence grew thick with the unknown—with danger. Cade woke from a sound sleep, his instincts humming.

Bayleigh had fallen asleep on top of him, their bodies still joined, and he disentangled himself and rolled her to her side gently—not making a sound to alert the intruder. He grabbed the Ruger he knew she kept in the nightstand and felt around on the floor for his own weapon before moving into the main part of the house.

He was naked as a baby, but it went unnoticed. Adrenaline surged through his body, his only thought protecting Bayleigh. He wouldn't lose her, no matter the cost.

He stopped in the hallway and listened for even the slightest sound. There was none, but he knew someone was there. The smell of coffee had him slowing his steps and letting out a relieved breath. He saw Declan's outline in the darkness of Bayleigh's kitchen. The man didn't make a sound as he prepared two cups of coffee and set them on the table.

"Sorry to interrupt," Declan said, holding up the clothes Bayleigh had left lying around, his dark brows raised high in question.

"You didn't," Cade growled, grabbing the clothes and taking them back to the bedroom with him.

He pulled on his jeans before going back to meet with his brother. Dec wouldn't have come unless there was an emergency, and Cade had a sinking feeling in his gut he knew exactly what he was here for.

"They found Becca Whitson's body," Declan said.

Cade sat down across from his brother and took the cup of coffee Dec passed him, drinking down the hot, bitter liquid with a long swallow.

"Was it like the others?" he asked.

"Yeah, with a few new additions to the scene." Dec pulled out a file folder and slid it across the table. "Becca Whitson looks an awful lot like Bayleigh. They have the same coloring, though they're built a little differently."

"I've never seen the girl, but I know Bayleigh was fond of her. She'd been a client for a while, but she'd just recently gotten engaged. Bayleigh was designing a large trousseau for her honeymoon."

Cade looked through the photos taken at the crime

scene. There was no point in asking how Declan had gotten the photos and information so quickly. His brother had connections that boggled Cade's mind.

"Shit," Cade said.

His gut clenched at the sight in front of him. The soldiers Carlos had sent for Becca hadn't been kind to her. But it was the pictures scattered around the crime scene that boiled his blood. He'd known they'd watched the morning Bayleigh had come to him in his garage.

The pictures showed them both clearly—Bayleigh pressed against the wall, her head thrown back in ecstasy while his fingers were buried inside of her. There were other pictures of her scattered around as well—pictures of her inside of her shop, going for coffee, and jogging around the neighborhood. Carlos couldn't have made it any clearer that Bayleigh was his next target.

"I can take her in, Cade. Put her in a safe house until the cartel is destroyed. Carlos is coming after her. And the word came in from Homeland Security about an hour ago that Miguel del Fuego died from whatever drug was slipped to him. Carlos is in charge of the whole operation now. Let me protect her."

Cade threw down the photos and stared harshly at his brothers. "No. She's mine. I won't trust her safety with anyone else."

"You're not thinking straight. I swear I won't let anything happen to her. I'll see to it myself. I won't let anyone else you love be hurt. I didn't get there in time to save Carmen, and I regret that every day."

Cade raked his fingers through his hair and massaged the stiff muscles at the back of his neck. "There's nothing you could have done. You're not fucking Superman. And you're wrong about Bayleigh. I don't love her. It's not like that. But I'm responsible for her. I knew from the beginning that anyone I was interested in would become an automatic target of the cartel. She was bait, plain and simple. Once Carlos made it clear that he had her in his sights, I didn't have any choice but to draw her in closer to me. I needed to be able to keep an eye on her all the time."

"So you're saying you fucked her for her own safety?" Dec asked with a snort.

"Pretty much."

***

Bayleigh clasped her hand over her mouth and hunched over as the pain of Cade's words assaulted her. Her body jerked as if she'd received a physical blow, and shock kept her eyes dry even as her hands trembled.

Clear thought wasn't possible. All she knew was that she had to escape. She couldn't face Cade again. Not after she'd bared her soul to him. Not after he'd taken, no demanded, she give it to him.

She ran back into the bedroom as quietly as possible and pulled on a pair of black yoga pants, an old college sweatshirt, and flip-flops. The backpack in her closet held a change of clothes, extra keys and cash. Her brothers had made sure to instill the importance of always being prepared into her once she'd moved out on her own. She'd never thought she'd need it, but she was glad she'd listened to their advice.

The blinds of her bay window were pulled down thanks to Cade's paranoia, and she raised them slowly, putting her hand at the bottom and guiding them up so no noise would be made. She pulled the latch to the window and pushed it open, slipping out in the space between their two houses and staying to the shadows under the eaves.

She'd heard Cade say that he had men watching the house, and she knew the cartel he'd mentioned also had people watching. Stupid didn't even begin to describe how she felt. She'd been attracted to him from the start, and she'd gone into the affair with her eyes wide open, but that didn't make his words hurt any less. She was bait to destroy the cartel who'd killed the woman he really loved. He'd told her what he could give, and she'd thought she could change him. Lesson learned. There was no one to blame but herself.

The trees seemed to close around her as she ran away from her home. Away from Cade. She used her cell phone to call a cab and gave the location she wanted to be picked up. It would take her another ten minutes to reach it at a jog, so the timing would be right.

She didn't need either of the MacKenzies to protect her. She could protect herself. And if she felt she was in danger all she had to do was put a call in to her brother. Of course, if Brant and Cade were as close as Cade had said, then she was sure that Brant would give away her hiding place if Cade asked him to.

It didn't matter. The only thing that was important was that she separate herself from Cade and whatever he was involved in. She wouldn't be any man's burden. And she wasn't a victim. She'd had enough of men trying to tell her what to do in her life. Now all she had to decide was where she was going.

***

"Does it make you feel better to lie to yourself?" Declan asked. "You can't sit there and tell me that you don't love that woman."

"Why are you pushing this, Dec?" Cade scooted his chair back and went to get another cup of coffee, not wanting to face the sympathy he saw in his brother's face.

"Because you're an idiot. And because you deserve to be happy. What are you really afraid of here, Cade?"

He braced his arms on the counter and lowered his head, knowing that he could keep denying what he felt all he wanted, but that didn't mean it would go away.

"Dammit," Cade swore, rubbing his palms against his eyes. "You want to know what the hell I'm afraid of?" he demanded, his voice an angry whisper. "I feel guilty because what I felt for Carmen doesn't even come close to what I feel for Bayleigh. It makes me wonder if I even know what love really is. If I ever knew. What if I let myself love Bayleigh the way she deserves to be loved, and then she's taken from me? I can't even imagine the pain of losing Bayleigh, because what I feel for her is so much more."

"Do you really think you have a choice of *letting* yourself love her?" Dec asked, leaning back in his chair on two legs, his gaze steady and sober. "If you didn't love her already you wouldn't be struggling with yourself. And telling yourself that you don't love her won't make the pain lessen if something does happen to her. It's all about the time that you have and making the most of it."

Declan dropped his chair to the floor and gathered the file, before standing to leave.

"So now that you've decided to stop being a dumbass, it still doesn't change the fact that Bayleigh's in danger. If you won't send her to a safe house, the only other option is to use her as bait like you originally planned."

Cade turned around and crossed his arms over his bare chest, his muscles tensing as the words were spoken aloud. He'd already come to the same conclusion, but having Declan say them didn't make them any easier to swallow. It was time for Carlos and the cartel to be taken apart once and for all.

"Time's wasting," Dec said. "One of the men we captured finally broke and gave us some information. Let's draw him out."

He nodded once at Declan and went to get Bayleigh so she could hear Declan's plan. But he knew as soon as he entered the bedroom that she was no longer there. The bed was mussed, sheets twisted, from where they'd made love only a short time before. And it *had* been making love. He'd felt it all the way to his soul with the way she'd moved over him, bewitched him and given him everything he'd ever desired.

"Fuck." He looked into the bathroom and through her closet, but there was no trace of her. She'd run. From him. The feeling didn't sit well.

He felt Dec come in behind him, his cell phone already pressed to his ear as he talked to some unknown agent, giving the details of Bayleigh's escape and to alert anyone working the case to be on the lookout for her.

Cade pulled on his shirt and shoes and strapped on his weapon, grabbing his own cell phone and dialing Bayleigh's number. But it rang once and then went to voicemail. Panic clawed inside him as he thought of everything that could happen to her. She had no idea what a man like Carlos was capable of. And if he lost her, there would be no one to blame but himself.

CHAPTER FIFTEEN

The farther she got from Cade, the more worried Bayleigh became. The urge to run back to him hammered at her skull until a headache pounded in her temples. Cade might not love her, but he'd sworn to keep her safe, and she was being stupid taking off if there was even a hint of danger. Her family had taught her better than that. But a mix of pride, anger, and heartbreak had clouded her thinking.

No matter what her situation was, she didn't want to face Cade again. Her embarrassment was too great. But she knew she needed protection. Her only option was to call Brant and ask him for his help. And his silence.

The back of the cab was stuffy and she kept an eye on her surroundings as they made their way downtown. She didn't have a ton of cash on her, just enough to get by for a couple of days, so she couldn't stay somewhere extravagant.

Ring after ring echoed in her ear as she waited for Brant to pick up the phone. His terse voice came over the line, directing the caller to leave a message and she sighed in frustration.

"Brant, it's me," she said, wondering exactly how much to tell him. "I know you're friends with Cade, but—" Her breath hitched at the mention of his name, and she had to fight for control. "I need your help. I think I'm in trouble, and you're the only one I can ask. Just—call me back. Please."

She hung up the phone and blinked her eyes rapidly as tears threatened. They were in a crowded part of the city, and she saw the familiar sign of a motel coming up, the nightly rate flashing in red under the logo.

"Stop here, please," she said, pulling the cash from her bag and paying the driver.

Bayleigh paid cash for the room, and gave a random name to the girl behind the counter. Since she was paying in cash she didn't have to leave ID or credit card, and she asked for a second floor room close to the front office, thinking the more exposure she had the safer she'd be.

Her phone buzzed in her pocket and she pulled it out, seeing Cade's number flashing, and she pressed the mute button, cutting off his call. It was the third time he'd tried to reach her. Hopefully, he'd get a clue and stop trying. There was no way in hell she'd be talking to him any time soon.

The room was small and sparsely furnished—a queen-sized bed and a small desk and chair the only furniture—but it looked clean, at least on the surface. She made use of the coffee pot to warm her insides, hoping to soothe the uneasiness she felt at being out on her own.

Brant still wasn't answering, and she tossed her phone on the bed as she went into the bathroom. She showered quickly, leaving her hair wet since a blow dryer wasn't one of the room amenities, and she pulled on an oversized shirt. The phone on the bed showed she'd missed another call from Cade, but Brant hadn't tried to call her back. And he would have if he'd gotten the message.

The heavy blackout curtains were pulled tight, but she checked them and the door locks again before slipping beneath the scratchy sheets. Her mind wouldn't settle, and she tossed restlessly, trying not to think how empty the bed felt without Cade beside her. An uneasy sleep finally came over her, her body recognizing the need for rest even if her mind didn't.

***

Bayleigh couldn't say what woke her only a short time later. It wasn't a specific sound. More of a movement that didn't seem to belong in the stillness of her room. Her eyes popped open and she waited for them to adjust to the darkness. But they didn't. To adjust there had to be at least a small amount of light coming from somewhere.

The room was black as pitch, as if she were inside a sealed tomb, and panic began to claw its way out as disorientation played tricks on her mind. Not even the heater made a sound as the silence covered her like a heavy blanket, smothering the shreds of her sanity.

"Good, you're awake," an amused voice said, his Latin

accent smooth. "We have so little time together, I thought it would be best to get started right away."

A match flared and her eyes were drawn to the flame as it lit the candles on each side of the bed. A burst of panicked laughter bubbled in her throat at the thought that her kidnapper was trying to be romantic, but he quickly set her straight.

"The second floor is on a separate fuse box than the first floor and the front office," he said conversationally. "It wasn't difficult to cut the electricity, especially since there are no other guests near you to complain."

Her eyes made the quick adjustment to the meager light, but she couldn't break her stare away from the madman in front of her. Carlos del Fuego would have been a handsome man if his black eyes hadn't held so much menace. He wasn't very tall—a couple of inches shy of six feet—but he was solidly built, muscular enough that it was obvious he worked out. His black hair was cut short, and his clothes were expensive and well tailored. He didn't look like a killer. Except for the eyes. Those eyes couldn't conceal the kind of man he was.

God, she had to think, but terror was building inside of her like nothing she'd ever experienced, and she felt frozen, trying to remember the advice her brothers had given her. She'd never had to fight off an attacker before, and practice was a hell of a lot different than the actual event.

She squeezed her eyes closed and slowed her breathing, trying to gather her thoughts and decided what she should do.

"Now, now," Carlos said, his chuckle grating across her spine. "Open your eyes, little one. I want to see your fear. It makes me hard."

He sat down on the bed beside her and she didn't take time to think as she rolled in the opposite direction, wanting nothing more that to put as much space as possible between them. Her shoulder bumped the bedside table, making the candle wobble precariously, and one leg slid to the floor, but he was too fast. His hands clamped around her arms, his fingers biting into her skin painfully, and she cried out as he jerked her back up to the center of the bed.

His strength was overwhelming as he restrained her arms as easily as if she were a small child. She fought against him impotently as he did the same thing to her legs, binding each one to the corners of the bed. She opened her mouth to scream, but he shoved a thick piece of cloth past her lips, quickly muffling her efforts.

She looked around frantically, trying to think through the panic, but she was completely at his mercy. The thick curtains had been taped down against the wall and down the seam so outside light couldn't get in, and he'd re-bolted the door after he'd gained entrance. She had no idea how he'd gotten inside, especially since she hadn't heard him make a sound.

"It is interesting to see all of your thoughts flash across your face," he said. "You are wondering how I came to be in here." His smile was sinister, the white of his teeth flashing between full lips that any woman would kill for. "All I can say is that there are perks to growing up surrounded by criminals. It's an education you can't get in normal surroundings."

Bayleigh tried to slow her breathing so she didn't pass out, but she wasn't having much luck with the cloth stuffed inside her mouth.

"There's no escape for you now." He unzipped his leather jacket and tossed it across the desk, leaving him in a plain white t-shirt that stretched around his biceps. "I guess it serves you right for selling your body to that bastard."

Anger flashed in his eyes, and she assumed the *bastard* was Cade. Carlos lifted the leg of his jeans and pulled a wickedly sharp knife from the leather sheath strapped to his calf. Her eyes widened in fear as he turned the blade slowly so she could see the gleaming curve of it in the candlelight.

"You see this, *puta*?" he asked. "I'm going to take that gag out of your mouth, and if you make one sound, I'm going to start cutting. Do we understand each other?"

Bayleigh nodded frantically, praying for a miracle. He pulled the wadded cloth from her mouth, and she swallowed, her mouth dry with fear.

"Cade will come for you," she said, wishing she'd slept in her clothes instead of the thin t-shirt and panties she wore. "He'll kill you."

"If that traitor cared for you at all he would have put a tracker on you like I did," Carlos said, holding up her phone. "It wasn't hard to slip into the house and put in the chip while you were visiting the lady across the street. Like I said, I've got talents the men who were watching your house could never dream of."

He reached into his jacket pocket and pulled out a pair of surgical gloves, blowing into each one before putting his hands inside, as if he'd done it a thousand times before. Once the gloves were on he pulled out a small vial of white powder, no bigger than her pinky finger, from his pocket.

"Cade MacKenzie has been a problem for me," Carlos said. "He turned my father against me. He gained the respect of the cartel soldiers until they only listened to his orders and questioned mine. He seduced my sister and got her killed, and he destroyed our original labs with the information he held. We lost millions of dollars of this powder you can't keep your eyes off of. And all the while, MacKenzie was really working for his government."

"Good," Bayleigh said, her eyes flashing as the fight returned to her body. There was no way in hell she was just going to lie there helplessly and let him kill her. If she was going to die, then she'd do it fighting with her last breath. "You seem to be under the impression that the bad guys are supposed to win. I'm going to enjoy watching him take you apart."

"He can try," Carlos sneered. "But that won't change the fact that you'll be dead. This is payback. I've got men taking care of Cade's sister as we speak. And I've got you all to myself. I only wish he could be here to see how much you suffer." He shrugged as if Cade's absence were a minor inconvenience. "He'll find your body, and that will have to be enough."

Bayleigh bit back a scream as he brought the knife up and sliced down the center of her shirt, the sharp blade cutting through the fabric like water. She couldn't help the shudders that wracked her body as he looked her over, his gaze stopping at her breasts hungrily before moving down to the lacy white panties she wore. She glared at him, twisting her wrists against the restraints, not caring as they bit into her skin.

"MacKenzie always did seem to have all the luck." Carlos' eyes darkened with lust and he reached out to tweak her nipple, laughing as she cringed away from him. "I wish I had more time to enjoy you."

Carlos uncorked the small vial and stuck the tip of his pinky inside so only a small amount of white powder clung to his finger.

"You cringe from me now, but you'll be screaming my name before I'm finished with you."

"The hell I will," she spat.

Unbidden tears filled her eyes as he rubbed the white powder down the center of her chest, rubbing it into her skin almost lovingly.

"It'll always be his name," she said viciously as her body began to tighten, the familiar prickle of arousal slithering across her skin. "You may take my body, but it'll be him I'm thinking of."

***

"Where the hell is she?" Cade asked Declan as his brother got off the phone with one of his men. "Fuck, I can't just stand here waiting." He paced across his living room, waiting for his brother to give him news.

There was only about an hour left until sunrise, and she'd already been gone too long. The phone call he'd gotten from Carlos an hour before had sent all of the agents in the area scrambling. They had to find Carlos before he followed through on his threat to kill Bayleigh. Because once he killed Bayleigh, Carlos would be in the wind until he found the perfect opportunity to go after Cade himself. This was the last chance they had to get him before he disappeared again.

He and Dec had traced Bayleigh's steps to the other side of the trees into an open field, where the land was being leveled for a new subdivision. There was no trace of her once she left the sandy area, which meant she had transportation of some kind. Or worse, she was forced to take transportation of some kind. But he didn't think so.

Carlos had let it slip during his phone call that he had a tracker on her, and that he'd been on his way to her even as they spoke. They *had* to find her before Carlos got a hold of her. Her chances of surviving lessoned if he had her in his possession.

Cade tried not to let the panic overwhelm him, but it was getting more difficult with every second that passed. His training was the only thing keeping him sane. He couldn't lose her now.

"That was the cab company," Declan said. "They picked up a woman matching Bayleigh's description about five blocks from here. I've got an address. Let's go."

Cade's phone rang as he climbed into Declan's Jeep and he looked at the number. A muttered curse escaped his lips and he knew he was in deep shit. He wouldn't have even answered it if it weren't for the fact that Darcy might be in trouble.

"MacKenzie," he said, holding onto the dash as Dec took a corner at high speed. A couple of unmarked agency vehicles followed close behind them as they weaved in and out of what little traffic was on the road at that time of night.

"What the *fuck* is going on there?" Brant yelled through the phone.

"We've got her location. We'll get to her."

"You shouldn't have let her go in the first place, asshole. She was fucking crying when she left the message on my phone. She never cries. If things hadn't been going to shit here when she called I would have been able to talk to her to find out what the hell you did to her. But whatever it is, apologize and get her back under your protection."

"Is Darcy okay?" he said, slanting a look at Declan. "What happened?"

"She's fine. And the men Carlos sent are taken care of. A cleanup team will be here to get rid of them in a couple of hours. I'll take care of Darcy because I promised I would. Now you take care of Bayleigh, or I'll fucking kill you. Best friend or no."

The phone went dead and Cade tossed it into the seat beside him, frustration and impotent rage eating at him.

"Can't you go any faster," he yelled. "Dammit."

His fist pounded against the dash and he welcomed the

pain that sang in his hand. He didn't think he'd ever been so terrified in his entire life. Not even when he'd been looking into Miguel del Fuego's eyes when he'd killed his own daughter. Bayleigh was everything to him. She was his life and his future. He couldn't even consider that he wouldn't get to her in time. He just had to. Plain and simple.

They pulled into a motel parking lot that was more than half empty, and Cade was out of the Jeep and running toward the office before it rolled to a complete stop. Declan grabbed him from behind, his arms tightening like a vise around him before he could burst into the office and terrify the girl behind the counter.

"You've got to calm down and think straight," Declan hissed in his ear, "Or I swear to God I'll find enough men to sit on you while I go in. Priority number one is making sure she's safe. You'll endanger that if we don't do this as a team."

Cade nodded once and shook him off, unholstering his weapon and checking the clip. "What room?" he asked. "Now Declan. You and I do this now, or I go in alone."

"212," he answered, taking out his own weapon and following Cade up the stairs.

Declan made hand signals to a couple of the other agents and sent them around to the back of the building, and he had two more wait as back up outside the door.

Cade and Declan got in position at each side of the dark blue door, the number *212* nailed at the center in tarnished bronze. His body tensed as adrenaline pumped through his veins in time with his heart. He couldn't afford to think the worst. His focus had to be complete and he blanked his mind and let his training take over, waiting for Declan to give the signal to enter.

Or he'd *planned* on waiting. At least until he heard the thin, mewling whimper through the door. All bets were off then, and his control dissolved. The only thing in his head was the need to protect. She was *his* woman.

Cade's foot kicked against the thin door and he vaguely heard Declan's curses as it crashed open. It took a second for his eyes to adjust to the darkness of the room, but he'd never forget the sight in front of him for as long as he lived. Carlos stood by the bed, his body naked and erect, preparing to crawl between Bayleigh's legs as tears streamed down her face. Her head shook in denial even as her eyes gleamed with lust and her body was ready for the taking.

Cade let Declan take the fatal shot, knowing his control was in shreds, and he didn't want Bayleigh to see the side of him that could kill so easily. He spared a glance as blood bloomed across Carlos' chest, and he collapsed across the bed. The team of agents Dec had with him went into action, but his eyes were only for Bayleigh. He holstered his weapon and went to her, kneeling beside her and working at the knots at her wrists.

"He drugged her," Declan said, averting his eyes from her naked body.

"Bayleigh," Cade said. "Let me help you, sweetheart."

He pulled the disheveled sheets across her body as she

cringed away from him.

"Don't touch me," she pleaded. "I can't fight it if you touch me. It hurts too bad."

The knots at her ankles were tighter, and Cade used the knife Declan tossed him, cutting her free quickly.

"Ssh, it's okay, baby. Just relax. I've got to get you out of here before the drug gets all the way into your system. Hold on a bit longer for me."

He rolled the sheets around her and lifted her in his arms. She moaned lustily, her body shifting against him, searching for a fulfillment she hadn't wanted but was left with no choice but to take. She bit at his neck, her tongue stroking in hot little licks against his skin.

"Bayleigh, you've got to control it," he said desperately, even as his body tightened.

He wouldn't take her like this. Couldn't take her like this. But he knew if she didn't find relief soon then the pain would get worse until she could lose her sanity. The drug was still untested enough that the effects were different for everyone, though as long as it had been given to her topically she was in no danger of death like with an internal dose.

Declan handed him the keys to the Jeep. "Get her out of here. I'll grab a ride with one of my men. We've got the location of several of the cartel members, and a few others in questioning. Hopefully one of them will have information on the labs where this shit is developed."

Cade nodded and headed out the door and down the

stairs before anyone could stop him to talk. He saw patrol cars pulling up late to the party, his captain stepping out of one of them with a narrow-eyed glare that had Cade wincing. He was going to get a hell of a tongue-lashing from every boss he had, local and federal. But it just couldn't be helped. Bayleigh was his first priority. The rest of them could wait. Or better yet, he could resign for real and tell everyone to kiss his ass. That was sounding like the more prudent course of action.

He sat Bayleigh in the passenger seat gently and put a hand to her brow. Her face was flushed and dewed with perspiration, and her eyes were wild, searching for someone—anyone—to give her what she needed.

"Hang on, baby."

He ran around to the other side and started the Jeep, speeding out of the parking lot and heading back in the direction of their houses. He didn't know if she could last the fifteen minutes it would take to give her privacy.

"Cade, please," she cried. "I ache."

"I won't take you like this, baby. Not when you don't even know it's really me."

"I know it's you," she panted. "You're an asshole. But you're all I've got at the moment. If I don't come soon I'm going to die. And then you can go jump off a cliff. It's my turn to use you for a change."

His heart clutched at her words, knowing for sure now that she'd overheard that part of his conversation with Declan. He needed to explain, to tell her he'd been a fool.

But not until she could understand him clearly. He was actually surprised she was as coherent as she was. Carlos either didn't give her a large enough dose, or Bayleigh was putting up one hell of a resistance. He had a feeling it was the latter.

She shrugged out of the sheet and scooted across the bench seat until she was practically straddling his thigh.

"Fuck, Bayleigh," he said, swerving to miss a car as she blocked his view of the road.

Her hands were busy, working at the buckle of his belt and unzipping him with record speed. He cursed his body, wishing he had enough control over his cock to tell it not to spring to life every time she touched him, but he'd never in a million years have control like that. Only a saint would.

"Stop, baby. We'll be home in a few minutes."

Her hot hands grasped around him and he sucked in a hard breath, his foot pressing down on the gas until he was breaking so many laws he didn't want to think about the consequences. His arm curved around her body and her knees straddled his thigh so she was open to him, and he plunged two fingers inside of her from behind. She screamed and bit his shoulder as she clamped around him and came in an instant.

His eyesight dimmed as she stroked him while her hot body writhed. Sweat popped out on his forehead as he felt the first signs of his own orgasm. Their street came into view and he breathed a sigh of relief, taking the corner on two wheels. He was damned glad it was in the middle of the night and all the busy-bodies on the street would be tucked into bed. There was no way he could get them both inside his house circumspectly.

"More, more," she chanted, over and over again.

He managed to get his foot on the brake, and skidded to a stop haphazardly in his driveway. Declan would retrieve the vehicle later. Cade had the wherewithal to grab the sheet and pull it around her as he lifted her out of the Jeep, her soaked pussy pressing against his cock, searching desperately for him as she tried to draw him inside.

"Dammit, Bayleigh. Stop it," his teeth snapped together as he tried to reposition her. "I'm not taking you like this. I'll make you come all you want, sweetheart, but I can't do this to you. Not until you're ready to listen to me."

He stumbled through his front door, their balance precarious, and he slammed it behind him with his foot. Her mouth clamped on his, hot and wet, as she bit at his lips, invading his senses as she alternated between languid strokes of her tongue and biting nips.

Her legs tightened around his waist and they spun so she was pressed against the wall. He needed to get back in control. Somehow. Jesus, she was making him crazy.

"Fuck me, Cade." She pulled at his shirt until she had it over his head and tossed to the floor. "I'm begging you."

"Bedroom," he rasped. "I'll take care of you, baby."

She threw her head back and moved against him, the hard bud of her clit sliding up and down his cock. He was going to be sore tomorrow, but there was pleasure with the pain, and he held back his own release as she came apart again in his arms.

"Please." Tears coursed down her cheeks, and her eyes were tortured with need. "I need you inside me. It's all I've ever needed. Don't deny me this. Just one last time and we can go our separate ways."

He couldn't bear her pain—pain that he'd caused her deep inside that had nothing to do with the drug Carlos had given her.

"Look at me, Bayleigh," he said, holding her face between his hands and forcing her to look him in the eyes. Her pupils were dilated to the point that the blue no longer showed. "I won't take you without you knowing the truth. I love you, sweetheart. With everything I am."

She fought against his hold as sobs wracked her body, even as her hips continued to thrust against him.

"Don't, Cade. Just sex. It's okay."

"Bullshit." His cock nudged against the entrance of her folds, but he held himself back, needing her to acknowledge what he needed to give her. "It was never just sex. And I'll be damned if this is the last time. I want you forever, Bayleigh."

He slammed inside of her, his control past the breaking point. There was no way he would be able to hold back his orgasm. She was slick and hot around him, and he hammered into her as orgasm after orgasm rolled through her body. His balls tightened and he pushed into her one last time as the most powerful climax he'd ever experienced wracked his body. His knees buckled and he managed to go to the floor without crushing her.

The wood was cold beneath his back, but Bayleigh was hot on top of him, their breaths racing like steam engines, and exhaustion was warring with the need. He knew they weren't done. It would take several hours for the drug to work its way through her system. As soon as she came out of the doze she was in, she'd be ready for more.

CHAPTER SIXTEEN

The late morning sunlight streamed through the blinds, and Cade watched the play of shadows across the walls from the trees that blew with the rising wind. There would be a storm before long, inside as well as outside. There was too much between them that needed to be settled.

He'd managed not to drown them in the shower a half hour before, but it had been a close call. Hopefully, Bayleigh would be able to rest now—completely—with no nightmares of Carlos creeping up on her.

"I'm tired," she muttered against his shoulder.

He turned his head to look at her. She still had her eyes closed, but the flush of perpetual desire had finally left her skin, and now she was pale as the moon. Dark circles rested under her eyes and her hair was mussed and tangled around her face. He'd never seen her looking more beautiful. Just the fact that she was alive was a miracle in itself.

Her announcement was so ridiculous that he would've laughed if he'd had the energy. "You should be," he said. "I think I'm paralyzed from the waist down."

"You'd better not be." She tried to lean up on her arms, but didn't have the strength to hold herself up long. "I've got to get home, and I need someone to carry me. Since you're the only one here, I'm voting you for the job."

His fingers tightened against her back as her words slammed against him. "Bayleigh," he said. "I don't want you to leave. Stay with me. Make your home with me."

She tried to roll out of his arms, but the lethargy was too great, and he was able to stop her easily. He pinned her to the bed and made her look him in the eyes. There was no hiding now. He showed her everything that was swirling inside of him. Feelings he'd never let anyone else see.

"Don't do this, Cade," she said, her eyes filling with tears. "Let's just chalk this up to a learning experience and move on. I don't need you to say things you don't mean because you think you've hurt my feelings. I'm fine, but I need to move on. It's no big deal."

"The hell it isn't," he growled. "You said you loved me, Bayleigh. Was it a lie?"

She swallowed audibly, and her gaze drifted to his shoulder. The vulnerability that flashed in her eyes made him want to kick himself. He'd done nothing but hurt her since they'd met. All because of his insecurities and fears. He needed more than anything to hear her say those words again.

"No." The word was barely audible. "It wasn't a lie. I love you. That won't ever change."

He breathed a sigh of relief and bowed his head so it rested against her forehead.

"You left me too soon," he told her. "You didn't hear all of what I said to Declan. I was running scared, baby, and I was trying to come up with any reason I could to keep denying what I felt for you. It didn't take me long to realize that me denying it didn't make it untrue."

She tried to blink the tears back, her determination to not let him see her cry obvious. He remembered what her brother said. Bayleigh never cried. But it seemed that was all he'd made her do since he'd crushed whatever had been building between them with his callous words.

"I love you, Bayleigh. I mean every word of it. And I'll mean it forever. The thought of losing you is almost paralyzing, and I can't live without you."

He leaned down and kissed her softly. Desire was a distant simmer, and all that was between them now was the love they had for each other. She lost the battle with her tears and they escaped, trailing slowly down her pale cheeks.

"Marry me, Bayleigh. Make me alive again. Be my future."

Her arms tightened around him in a fierce embrace, and her "yes" was barely audible.

"Though I should probably make you suffer more," she said, her smile wobbly.

"Undoubtedly. But if it makes you feel any better your brother has threatened to kick my ass."

Her laughter brought joy into his heart—a joy he hadn't felt in so long he couldn't remember the last time. He held the woman he loved in his arms, knowing that he'd be able to face anything as long as she was by his side.

"I'll protect you," she whispered. "Always."

"Always," he promised.

EPILOGUE

Brant Scott stared at the bedroom ceiling, his heart still pounding and his cock still hard, as if he hadn't already had two of the most powerful orgasms he'd ever experienced.

Darcy was curled around him, her thigh thrown over his leg and her hand resting low on his stomach. He could tell by her breathing that she was already asleep, and he tried not to think about how good she felt in his arms. How *right* she felt there.

This was a mistake. Two people thrown into a high-tension situation who'd needed an adrenaline outlet. That was all.

He'd known he would leave her even as he'd given into the temptation of that tight little body. He'd put up with her taunts, sharp tongue and dry wit until he'd had no choice but to silence her with his mouth or go crazy. And damned if she hadn't matched his heat with her own, until he'd been all but dizzy with lust, ripping the clothes from her body like an animal and thrusting inside of her before they even managed to get inside the house.

Christ, just the thought how out of control it was made him want to turn her over and take her again. She did that to him. Made him lose every shred of control he'd ever had. And he'd vowed a long time ago that he'd never let another woman get to him that way. His first wife had taught him that lesson well enough.

Brant ignored the need in his body and slipped from beneath the covers, pulling them back up so Darcy wouldn't get cold, and he touched her cheek once with the tip of his finger. The regret inside him stronger than he wanted to admit.

His clothes were nowhere in sight, and he rolled his eyes, remembering they were still on the front lawn. He had to get out of here. He'd already gotten the call earlier that he was needed for another assignment. The sooner he cut ties the better.

Darcy wasn't a clinging woman. She'd understand what happened between them was nothing more than insanity, and never give it another thought. At least, that's what he told himself. She might be hurt that he hadn't said goodbye, but she'd understand. They were bound to see each other in the future, but he knew they'd be able to get through it without too much awkwardness.

Brant closed Darcy's front door behind him and began gathering his clothes, ignoring the tightness in his chest. This was for the best, he kept telling himself over and over again as he dressed quickly.

His Jeep sported a couple of new bullet holes thanks to Carlos del Fuego's men, but it still purred to life when he turned the key in the ignition. Brant fought the urge to look behind him as he drove away, but if he had, he would have seen Darcy at the window, the innocence that had once shone in her eyes shattered.

ABOUT THE AUTHOR

Liliana Hart is the pseudonym for an author of more than a dozen books. She lives in Texas with her husband and cats, and loves to be contacted by readers.

Connect with me online:

http://twitter.com/Liliana_Hart

http://facebook.com/LilianaHart

www.lilianahart.com

14202477R00124

Made in the USA
Lexington, KY
17 March 2012